SILVER SERIES

**SUPERB WRITING
TO FIRE THE IMAGINATION**

Nell Coleman writes, 'I grew up believing in another world that existed alongside the one I could actually see, hear and touch. It wasn't a big deal. I didn't make up stories about it or try to describe it. I was content to know that it was there, that I was privileged to be aware of it, and that some time – perhaps when certain conditions were met – it would become as real to me as the boring world I had to endure every day. In fact, I confidently expected home, family and school to be revealed as some sinister, made-up place that I could thankfully leave behind!

'Fortunately (or unfortunately?) I became more sensible and practical with each passing year and it was only when I started to write *The Osmid Version* that I found the story leading me back to that time, and I began to wonder all over again if the every-day world was actually as real as it seemed!'

The Osmid Version is Nell Coleman's first published novel.

The
Osmid
Version

Nell Coleman

*Hodder
Children's
Books*

A division of Hodder Headline Limited

For Alasdair, Sean, Paddy,
Robbie and Bill

Chapter One

Each morning when Mark woke up he had to readjust his eyes. He lay there blinking, knowing that if he swung the bed even a little bit the Mother would come in with his pill and orange juice. She was nice and he liked her – but this was the only time of the day when his mind was clear and he could think his own thoughts and he wanted it to go on for as long as possible.

He wanted to think about Monk. Monk was small and brown and shabby. The only thing in the whole world that was not bright and gleaming-new. Once he must have been new. Once he must have been a bright new toy monkey with silky fur and two eyes. A birthday present?

He sighed. If only he could remember what that meant. Birthday . . . Once upon a time . . . Shadows and darkness . . . A time when there were no suns in the sky . . . Long ago . . . Long ago . . . But he didn't know what that meant either. There was only here and now. Here and now. Nothing else. Only the bright world of the four suns . . .

He held the soft toy body to him and rubbed his chin along its grizzled head. There was a strange lump where the left eye had been. He fingered it and a word floated into his mind. 'Mended'. The monkey had been mended. It was not a word that anyone else used and Mark kept it secret to himself and only thought about it at this time in the morning when his mind was free.

The ridge of stitching pulled one side of Monk's face up into a smile – but it was still a sad, crooked face. Mark held him out at arm's length and swung him from left to right – and all the time the one remaining black-bead eye dangled from its strand of scarlet thread.

Once Monk had been new. Once Monk had been mended. Once, long ago, there had been another world – and as long as Monk was looking at him Mark had the feeling that it was this bright world with the four suns that was not real and that he didn't belong here at all.

He looked around, raising his head gently so that the bed wouldn't rock. Yes, it was his own room all right. White walls. White curtains. White wardrobe. White chest of drawers. White lampshade. White table. White chair. Even his posters and the old cushion on the chair and the home-made rug with the rabbits on it.

Everything was there all right. White and shining in the light of the second sun. Why did no one ever draw the curtains? Why didn't he draw them himself? He blinked again and pulled the coverlet over his head. Shadows and darkness . . . Shadows and wonderful comforting darkness . . . He made a cave with his knees and lay there with his eyes open. Wondering. Trying to remember . . . Trying to picture Monk when he was new . . .

The toy was still lying on Mark's knees. For a moment it balanced on top of the coverlet. Then very slowly it toppled sideways and rolled off. Mark heard it hit the floor and sat up. But he had forgotten. He had moved too quickly. The bed was swinging. He heard the Mother's footsteps in the hall. The day had begun.

The Mother always wore brown. Mark wasn't sure if she was the same one who had always been there but he liked her anyway. She was soft and warm and didn't mind giving him a cuddle when no one else was about. She bustled in now with the orange juice in a small silver tumbler and the pill in a paper cup.

'Good morning, Mark. Did you sleep well?'

'Yes. Is it school today?'

Mark bounced up but the bed was quite still. The Mother smiled. 'No school today. Today is Sat. Take your pill.'

Mark held out his hand and she tipped the capsule into his palm and handed him the silver tumbler. He took a sip of the orange juice. He meant to swallow the pill but it slipped out of his hand and rolled down into the bed. The Mother hadn't noticed. Mark didn't want to upset her. He twitched the cover over it and finished the drink.

'I might go to Martin's after the film show,' he said.

The Mother turned to get his clean clothes out of the wardrobe.

'That's nice,' she said. She brought out some jeans and a shirt and sweatshirt and laid them on the bed. 'Don't be late for lunch. You know what happens when the pair of you get talking.'

Mark waited till she had left the room before he felt for the pill. He wasn't sure what it was for. He thought he had been taking one every morning for the whole of his life but it was difficult to be sure and when he asked the Mother she just smiled. He hugged Monk. That was why he liked the early mornings. Time seemed to be in order then. Yesterday was still clear. Still in the past but still real. By the time he was up and dressed time had become confused and even yesterday was hard to remember.

Long . . . and smooth . . . and yellow. He'd never really examined one of the capsules before. It looked dry and almost too big to swallow. The orange juice was all gone. He decided to keep the pill for later. Not in his pocket. Not in his drawers. Under the floorboards?

Under the floorboards was his secret hiding place. He kept all sorts of useful things there. String. His penknife. An underwater torch. A first aid kit. No one ever looked into the dark places. The pill would be safe enough there. He put it into the box with the sticking plasters and covered the loose floorboard with the rabbit rug. Then he got dressed.

The Father was already eating when he went downstairs. Cornflakes in the bowl. Three pieces of toast in the rack. Coffee bubbling on the stove.

The Mother filled a jug with milk. 'You'll be late,' she said. Didn't she ever eat?

The Father grunted and put down the paper. 'Late for the film show? Never! That's one thing you can count on, eh, Mark?'

Mark mumbled something through a mouthful of cereal.

'Don't speak with your mouth full!' The Mother fed more bread into the toaster.

'Didn't have film shows when I was a boy!' The Father lifted the paper again. 'You don't know how lucky you are!'

The light on the toaster blinked and Mark shut his eyes and went on chewing. He was sure all this had been said before.

As soon as he'd finished he excused himself and went upstairs. Sat was a good day. No school. Cinema in the morning. Town in the afternoon. He went into the bathroom to brush his teeth. He liked going to the cinema. Last week it had been Peter Sellers in *The Pink Panther*. He remembered how his friend Martin had laughed. Martin was a good friend. A bit fat and bossy perhaps, but . . .

Suddenly he stopped brushing. Last week? His startled face stared back at him. Nine o'clock in the morning and he could still remember last week? That was odd! He hung up his toothbrush and grinned at his reflection. This was going to be quite a day!

Chapter Two

The Father was out in the front garden mowing the grass. He guided the mower round the stunted rose bushes and the stand of pampas-grass. He was very proud of his pampas-grass.

'Have a good day!' he said without looking up.

'You too!' Mark kicked a pile of grass cuttings and ran for the bus.

'Good morning, Mark!' The Bus Driver smiled as Mark climbed aboard. 'Going to the cinema, are we?' The Bus Driver knew everyone. 'Good morning, Mrs Brown. Good morning, Ruth.'

Mark sat as far back as possible. The Driver was a Robot. All the Bus Drivers were Robots. He wondered how long he had known that. He always sat as far away from them as possible but no one else seemed to mind. No one else seemed to notice it at all.

The cinema was down on the seafront. Right behind the Brighton Centre. Mark could see his friends milling about in the entrance as he waited to cross the road.

'Hi, Mark!' Phil was trying to swing round a lamp post. 'You're late!'

'No, I'm not!' Mark ducked the flying feet. 'Hi, Martin!'

Martin sat on the steps and tried to look superior. 'They're not open yet.' he said to no one in particular.

Mark sat down beside him. Most of the boys from Miss Ritchie's class were there. Martin. Phil. Trevor . . .

'Stupid place,' said Trevor. 'Don't know why we come.'

'It's Sat. That's why,' said Martin. 'Sat – cinema. It's better than school!'

'Yeah!' Phil came and sat beside them. 'Why can't they let us in?' Phil's arms and legs always twitched when he couldn't get on with things. He jumped up again and rattled the gates. 'Hey! Open up! It's eleven o'clock!'

'No it isn't.' Martin looked at his watch. Trust him to know the right time. He knew everything. Plump and weak-sighted he might be – but nobody laughed at him. He held up one pudgy finger and they all waited. The finger was quite steady but all the rest of his body seemed to be quivering. It was always quivering. Not with nerves though. Certainly not with nerves. Mark watched and waited with the rest.

'Now!' The finger stabbed the air. They made a rush

for the gates and the Doorman came forward and unlocked them.

'Good morning, Martin. Good morning, Trevor. Good morning, Phil.'

And suddenly Mark knew that this cheerful man in the brown uniform and the hat with the gold braid was a Robot too. He wondered why he had never noticed it before.

Everyone scrambled into the cinema and fought for the best seats. Mark sat between Martin and Phil. He didn't like the idea of the Doorman being a Robot. Bus Driver . . . Doorman . . . How many more? He wondered if he should say something to the others.

But the music swelled up and the lights dimmed. Oh well. Perhaps later . . .

The curtains swung open and a beam of light shone out of the projection box as an unseen voice announced the show.

'*The Pink Panther!* Starring Peter Sellers!' Mark did a double take. Surely it was a mistake? He expected everyone to boo and whistle – but they were all cheering!

'Phil!' he whispered urgently.

'Shut up!' Phil pushed him away with a bony elbow. He tried the other side.

'Martin, haven't we just . . .'

9

But Martin had no time for him either. He was sitting bolt upright, his eyes fixed expectantly on the screen.

Mark let himself sink back in his seat. Was this today? Or was it last week? Everyone was acting as if they'd never seen the film before. But they had seen it! Last week and . . . Last week they had all queued outside the cinema and Martin had looked at his watch and . . . He was sure they had seen *The Pink Panther*. Peter Sellers . . . Inspector Clouseau creating havoc . . . 'That's my pistol pen! You have your own pistol pen!' He was sure he'd seen that gag before. Last week and the week before that and . . .

On one side of him Phil was cackling away. On the other, Martin was positively shaking with laughter. Not like Martin to be taken in like this. Why didn't he complain? He must know he'd seen the film dozens of times. Mustn't he?

But Martin showed no sign of complaining. Behind the silver-rimmed glasses his eyes were quite pink with laughter.

Another yell filled the cinema. Mark began to feel uncomfortable. They couldn't *all* be wrong. It must be him. He must have made a mistake. Like when you think you've been to a place before and you know you couldn't possibly have . . . He sat up again and tried to concentrate. Peter Sellers was so funny that he couldn't help laughing. But he seemed to know all the words before he heard them and each situation was depressingly familiar.

Half-way through there was an interval. Mark fought his way to the snack bar and bought a packet of crisps.

'Hey, Martin!' he said. 'We've seen this film before, haven't we?'

'Seen *The Pink Panther*? You're crazy!' Martin was trying to decide whether to buy a Swizzle or a Crispy Bar and wasn't interested in anything else. Mark went back to his seat and ate his crisps. 'Salt and Vinegar' it said on the packet but they didn't taste of salt and vinegar. They didn't taste of anything at all.

'Want the rest?' He held out the half-empty packet as Martin came back with the Crispy Bar and the Swizzle and a choc ice besides.

'Yeah, thanks!' Martin polished off the crisps in one go. 'Great film, isn't it?' He tore the wrapper off the choc ice. 'Want some?'

Mark shook his head. 'Say, Martin . . .' he began.

'Shhh!'

The lights dimmed and the second half began. It was as familiar as the rest.

Chapter Three

There was a rush for the bus stops after the show.

'Going home?' Trevor lived on the same bus route.

Mark hesitated. Maybe Trevor had noticed the Robots? Maybe he should ask him? No. He thrust his hands deeper into his pockets. No good asking Timid Trev. He would deny knowing his grandmother if it would get him out of trouble.

'I'm going with Martin,' he said.

Yes. Speak to Martin. That would be best. Martin was a good friend. Good to talk to. Not always practical – but that didn't matter. They liked the same things. Shared the same ideas. Get him off the *Space Mags* and the gingersnaps and they'd soon . . .

'Gingersnaps?' The sound of his own voice startled him.

'What?' Trevor blinked quickly – and then looked away.

Mark grinned. Silly to have spoken aloud. But why should he remember something as trivial as gingersnaps?

'See you on Sun then,' he said quickly.

'Yeah.' Trevor edged away. 'See you on Sun.'

They sorted themselves into orderly queues. Martin and Phil lived near each other and Mark went over to them. They were laughing at some of the jokes in the film and repeating them to each other. Mark waited. They *must* realize they'd seen it all before? Mustn't they?

'Phil . . . Stand still a minute, Phil. Haven't we seen this film before? You know. *The Pink Panther*? I just kept thinking all the time that . . .'

'You're mad!' said Phil. 'You think too much! Did you see that bit . . .' And he went off into Inspector Clouseau again.

No. No good saying anything to Phil. He never listened to anything. Best wait till he got Martin alone. Wait till they could talk.

There was no sign of the bus. He walked across the road and stood in one of the old Victorian shelters. Hove to the west. Brighton to the east. The Channel sparkling in the light of the second sun. Two piers stretching out from the shore like fingers. Well, that was all right then. Just as it should be. And yet . . .

Had the West Pier always been a deserted grey ghost? Had the life of the seafront always been drawn east towards Brighton? He wandered over the wide pavement and stared out at the blue water. Funny how

13

things were coming into focus.

Brighton. Yes. That's where the buzz was. In the arches underneath the Promenade. In the funny little streets that ran up to the town centre. Around the Palace Pier. Was there still the same smell of fish and chips and the garish lights and the loud music? Was it still the same as last Sat?

Last Sat . . . It wasn't exactly clear yet. Not all of it. Just odd bits of memory that kept popping into his head. He leaned on the turquoise railings. Gift shops and amusement arcades and outdoor cafes and pavement artists and tatooists and street musicians. All the things the Mother didn't approve of. Well, so what? He kicked an empty cigarette packet over the sea wall. She didn't know everything. He liked the lights and the loud music and the swirl of people and the candy floss and all the glamour and glitz . . .

He turned back to Kings Road. Still no sign of the bus. That was unusual. Buses usually ran on time . . . Usually? He grinned. Another memory? Like the gingersnaps? He strolled along a bit and looked down at the beach.

The water was blue with little white ripples lapping the shore. Windbreaks made patches of colour on the sand. Each windbreak — a family. The bucket and spade brigade. A Father lying with a newspaper over his face.

A Mother in a bathing suit. Two children making sand-castles. All happy. All smiling. Just like the posters.

Had his family ever played by the sea? He tried to remember as he crossed back to the Centre. The Mother without her brown dress? The Father in his shirt sleeves? It didn't seem very likely. And yet . . .

'Bus coming!' He ran to join his friends.

'Good morning, Martin. Good morning, Phil. Good show was it? You're coming along too, are you, Mark?' The Driver greeted each of them as they got on the bus. Mark would have gone to the back but Phil shoved him into a seat behind the Driver. Obviously Phil didn't realize the Driver was a Robot. Or didn't care. Mark settled back and looked out of the window. Maybe he was making too much of it.

There was a lot of traffic along Kings Road and the bus had to keep stopping. Lots of people too. Mark watched them scurrying across to the Sea Life Centre. Had they done this last Sat as well? And the one before that? But why? He pushed his brow against the cool glass of the window. Thinking wasn't his best subject. Best wait till he got to Martin's house. Martin was good at working things out. Best just sit on the bus and look out for the lights of the Palace Pier.

But somehow even the Palace Pier didn't seem as exciting as usual. The paintwork looked rusty. The spangle of lights didn't glow. The people seemed dull and lifeless. The music was just a whine. Maybe the Mother was right. He sniffed. The smell was quite appalling and he was glad when the bus turned sharply away from the seafront and up past the Pavilion.

At least that looked reassuringly familiar. Golden domes and minarets. Smooth lawns and flower beds. Tourists picnicking. Cameras flashing. Yes. That was how it always was. Just like the posters . . . Just like the posters of the families enjoying themselves on the beach? Funny. He didn't usually think like this. What was the matter with the day?

They had reached the Open Air Market and now the streets were busier. More people at the bus stops. More people getting on and off the bus. More comments from the Bus Driver.

'Goodbye, Mrs Brown. Goodbye, Michael . . . Hello, Mr Gilbert. Got the weekend shopping, have you?' Mr Gilbert clutched his parcels and sat down and the Driver smiled and swung the bus back into the stream of traffic.

Out past the Levels. Away from the shops. Away from the town. Now it was taking them past a group of tower blocks. Mark's father worked in one of them. Which one? He didn't know. They all looked the same. Tall and white and shining in the sunlight. The windows threw back images of yet more tower blocks. There was no way to see inside.

'Does your Father work in the towers?' he asked Phil.

'Nope. In a factory. I'll show you when we get there.'

'What does he do?'

Phil looked surprised. 'I never asked,' he shrugged.

'Haven't you ever been inside?'

'Not inside. They don't let anyone inside.'

'Don't you know what they make?'

Phil thought for a bit.

'It doesn't matter.' he said at last.

Mark sighed. He had a sudden longing for Monk. 'No! No way!' he told himself. 'That's all I need! Martin and Phil knowing I talk to a toy monkey? I'd never live it down! All the same. I could do with him now.'

'There it is!' Phil's elbow dug into Mark's side again. Mark winced. He wished Phil wouldn't always do that.

'What?'

'The factory, stupid! Where my Father works!' Mark looked out of the window. A heavy fence surrounded bright green lawns. The factory was made out of boxes. Huge orange boxes stacked on top of each other. Backed on to each other. Joined end to end like building blocks. From the centre an enormous chimney rose to the sky. There was no smoke and the gates were padlocked.

'It's shut!'

'Of course it's shut! It's Sat!'

Mark didn't know what to say. Yes, things were coming into focus all right – but why did none of it seem quite right? And why didn't anyone else seem worried about it? A factory made of boxes? Phil obviously thought it was OK. He glanced round and Martin grinned at him. He frowned. Martin could be annoyingly smug at times. But just wait till he could get him on his own! Martin didn't like other people knowing more than he did. He wouldn't like to think he'd been laughing at a film he'd seen – how many times before? Oh no! He wouldn't be quite so smug then!

Mark turned his attention to the scene outside. They'd left the centre of town now. Now they'd begun to climb.

They turned up Elm Grove and the Driver changed down a gear. Not so many people getting on now. Now they were all going home. Mark looked up at the Racecourse. Brighton was built on hills. Hollingbury. Whitehawk. Race Hill. Martin lived on Whitehawk. Right up near the top in one of the long tight rows of houses that clung to the contours of the land. Right and left, they stretched into the distance. But why did they all look the same? Why could you only see the fronts of the houses?

A concrete path. A front door. Three windows. Two

up and one down. Lace curtains. Bamboo blinds. Pot plants on the windowsills. Front gardens separated by low hedges. A wall running along the length of the road pierced only by little wooden gates. At the corner, another row of houses faced on to another street. Three windows. One door. Lace curtains. Bamboo blinds . . .

'What's at the back of your house?' he asked Martin.

'The back?'

'I can only see the fronts. What's the back like?'

'Why do you want to know?'

'I just thought . . . I've never seen the back.'

'You're crazy!' Martin rose and pressed the bell. 'Are you coming?'

'Yeah.' Mark pushed out of his seat. 'Bye, Phil!'

'Bye! See you on Sun!'

Mark followed Martin along the road and into his house. Now they could talk. But Martin's Mother was in the kitchen.

'Hello, Mark,' she said. 'Good film?'

'Yes, thank you,' said Mark politely.

'What was it today?'

'*The Pink Panther.*' Mark looked to see if there was any reaction. There wasn't.

'Eat your biscuits and go upstairs.' She brought out a tin of gingersnaps. Gingersnaps . . .? But this time Mark didn't even smile.

'Mark wants to see the back of the house,' said Martin.

'What for?' The Mother put down the tin and stared at him.

'I've . . . I've never seen the back.' Mark could feel his cheeks flushing.

'Do I come looking at the back of your house?' She tipped the biscuits on to a plate and handed it to him. 'Where's your manners?'

Mark took the plate and followed his friend upstairs. What was so bad about wanting to see the back of someone's house? Why did it matter suddenly? Just because Martin's Mother had managed to make him feel small? Well, he'd soon show *her*. He passed the plate to Martin.

'I need to go to the lavatory,' he said.

'OK. Don't be long though. I've got some new *Space Mags*.'

Mark locked the door behind him and looked around. There was only one small high window. Carefully, quietly, he put down the toilet seat and stood on it. More lace curtains. He pulled them aside. But the glass was thick and frosted and he could see nothing. The window was open at the top but he couldn't stretch any higher. He stood for a minute then climbed down and pulled the chain.

Martin's Mother was waiting for him on the landing.

'Well, Mr Nosey Parker?'

'I had to go to the toilet.' Mark could feel his face going red again.

'Huh!' she said noisily. 'You'd better go home.'

Martin came out of his room. Mark expected him to say something about the comics but he said 'Goodbye' instead.

Mark felt himself trembling inside. He'd been put in the wrong somehow and he couldn't explain it.

The Mother was holding the door open. There was nothing for it but to go home.

Chapter Four

Lunchtime. Mark sat between his parents and tried to eat his hamburger and chips. They didn't taste of anything either. What was the matter with the day? What was the matter with him?

'Not hungry, Mark?' The Mother looked at him anxiously.

'I guess not.' Mark put down his knife and fork. 'Can I go now?'

'What! No pudding?' The Father was clearing his plate. 'Why, at your age I was always starving! What have you been doing?'

'I went to the cinema.'

'Ah! The cinema! I bet you stuffed yourself!'

'I had a packet of crisps.'

'Just one packet?'

'I didn't finish them.'

'I'll bet!' The Father winked and helped himself to chocolate pudding. 'What did you see?'

'It . . . It was *The Pink Panther*.'

The Mother ladled some of the pudding on to a plate and put it in front of Mark. 'That's a good film. Did you enjoy it?'

Mark didn't know how to answer. He pushed at the brown stuff with his spoon.

'Your Mother asked you a question!' The Father was staring at him. They were both staring at him. Waiting. Mark slid the bowl away from him.

'Yes. It's a good film.'

'Want a lift into town, then?' The Father attacked his pudding with gusto. 'We men must stick together!'

'Yeah . . . OK . . . Thanks . . .'

Mark escaped upstairs. He needed to think things out.

From his bedroom window he could see nearly all the other houses on the estate. Each one floated in a sea of green lawn with its tuft of pampas-grass bobbing alongside.

'No walls. No fences. No secrets.' He picked Monk off the headboard and sat down on the bed with him. Perhaps now the day would start to make sense.

'What *is* at the back of Martin's house? Do you know?' No. No good expecting Monk to answer. All the same. It was good to be holding the old toy again. 'His Mother was really odd about it,' he went on. 'Martin was really odd. Not like him not to want to talk!' He sighed. 'The whole morning's been odd. Just a regular Sat – and yet . . . Why do I keep thinking it wasn't right? Not just the Robots! The film show – the crisps – the journey to Martin's house . . . But nobody else seems to notice!'

He hugged the monkey to him. 'Do you think it's me? My friends are always saying I'm crazy . . .' He rubbed his chin along the scarred monkey-face. 'But I'm not, am I? And nothing's different. It's just another day. Another Sat. I woke up. Got up. Got dressed. Went downstairs . . .' He looked around. The room was just the same. White walls. White curtains. White lampshade. White table. Rabbit rug . . .

Rug? Suddenly he was on his knees and clawing up the loose board. 'I didn't take the pill, did I? That's the only thing that's been different! I didn't take the stupid pill!'

He jumped up with the capsule in his hand. 'Long . . . and smooth . . . and yellow.' He sat down on the bed again. 'And the shell looks so thick! Must be something really horrible inside. Something they don't want you to taste. Maybe it burns your throat . . .'

He rolled the pill between his fingers. It was in two parts. They fitted closely together but if he pulled gently at each end . . .

'What did I tell you? Look at that!'

The powder had spilled on to his knee. It was silver. Shining silver grains with some specks of blue in it. Mark licked his finger and lifted some to his mouth.

'Yuck!' The bitterness made his eyes water and his tongue go dry, and when he looked down at his knee he saw with horror that the silver granules were burning into the denim.

'And they expect me to swallow that? No way!'

He ran to the bathroom and flushed the capsule and the powder down the lavatory.

'You all right, Mark?' It was the Mother.

'Yeah! OK!' Mark hurried back to his room. 'Better get rid of these!' He rolled the jeans into a bundle and stuffed them into the wardrobe. His good trousers were lying on the bed. He pulled them on and ran downstairs.

In a funny way he felt better now something had actually happened. Silly not to have kept the pill but at least now he had something real to tell the others. Now they would *have* to listen!

'Come on! I haven't got all day!' The Father was sitting in the car.

Mark did up his seat-belt and forced himself to relax. He couldn't wait to meet up with Martin and the others.

'This OK for you?' The Father stopped the car in the centre of town.

'Yeah. Thanks.' Mark hesitated. 'Are you really going to work?'

'Of course.'

'But it's Sat!'

'Got to keep the wheels turning!'

The Father leaned across and opened the passenger door. 'Have a good time. Don't be late home!'

The Father raised one brown-gloved hand as he drove off. Mark watched until the car disappeared and then turned towards the great open-air shopping centre of Churchill Square.

Then he stopped. It was Churchill Square all right. But . . . open air? He could feel the confidence of the last half hour draining away.

And yet . . . People were there, weren't they? Wasn't this the usual Sat afternoon crush? He took a few deep breaths. All those people couldn't be wrong! They were pouring off the buses, climbing up from the underground car park, flowing in from the street. The wide front plaza was teeming with them. Queues at the phone booths. Queues at the cash points. Goodness knows how many were crushed into the rest of the square. Yes. Martin and Phil and the others would be there. He was just being silly again. All he had to do was find them. He glanced up at the Telecom clock. Nearly half-past two. He was probably early. Well – they'd not be long. He dodged across Western Road and went into Smith's. Everybody went into Smith's sooner or later.

There didn't seem to be anything new at the magazine stand. Same old stories in *Melody*. Same old *Space Mags*. He wondered if Martin's had been any different. He was sure he'd seen everything in Smith's before.

Still no sign of anyone he knew. Dixons was next door but it was full. He went into the Record Hut instead.

There was a crowd of girls around the counter and they giggled as he passed. He couldn't understand why girls always had to be in groups and why they made that silly noise. It was all right while he was with his friends but when he was alone he didn't like it at all. He stuck his hands in his pockets and pretended not to notice.

A booth at the back of the shop was empty and he went in and sat down. There were three buttons. A red one, a blue one and a green one. Mark read the labels carefully. 'Kriss Killers.' 'Hocus Pocus.' 'Mantrax.' He put on the headphones and pushed the green button for Mantrax.

The sound was loud and discordant with a heavy beat. Mark didn't like it. He pushed the red button for

Kriss Killers but the sound continued as before. Red button, blue button. Red . . . blue . . . green . . . He tried dozens of different sequences but the same sound continued relentlessly.

The Assistant walked past. He smiled at Mark and Mark wondered if he should complain. The Assistants wore blue jeans and they were always smiling. Always smiling . . . Mark smiled back and the young man moved away.

A girl came out of a booth in front of him and Mark slipped in and took her place. Red button . . . blue button . . . green button . . . Kriss Killers . . . Hocus Pocus . . . Mantrax . . . It was still the same.

He walked slowly to the front of the store. Everyone else seemed happy enough. Their eyes were shining, their bodies pulsing to the beat. Why couldn't *he* hear music? The day was getting worse again. What was the matter with him? It couldn't really be because he hadn't taken the stupid pill, could it?

A girl that he knew was in one of the booths at the front of the shop. Janina. Mark leaned against the partition until she noticed him.

'Hi, Mark!'

'Hi! You been to the film show?'

'I go horse riding.'

'I forgot.'

'Heard Mantrax?'

Mark hesitated. Did he really want to hear that tuneless beat again?

'I'm waiting for a booth,' he muttered.

But Janina had made room for him on the stool. There was nothing for it but to squeeze in beside her.

'It's great!' she said handing him one of the headphones. Mark listened to the sound. It was the same as before but Janina was smiling at him and he could hear her feet tapping.

The Assistant walked past again. Smiling.

The Assistant smiled. Janina smiled. Mark tried to smile but his mouth wouldn't work. The Assistant couldn't possibly know he hadn't taken his pill? Of course he couldn't. But why was he always coming and looking at him? Why was he always smiling?

'There's a booth.' Janina took the headphones from him. 'Do you want to come swimming at the King Alfred this afternoon?'

'No.' Mark stumbled off the stool. 'I'm going to meet Martin.'

'It's good fun. They've got a new underwater grotto.' Janina was blue-eyed and pretty and she was smiling at him.

'I told you. I'm meeting Martin.'

She pouted at him and flounced out. Mark didn't

know what to say. He didn't really want to see Martin now. Or Phil. Or anyone. He just wanted to get home as quickly as possible. He made his way out of the shop and across the plaza and started walking up Dyke Road.

His mind was going round and round. Mantrax . . . blue button . . . red button . . . Kriss and *The Pink Panther* . . . Was this really Sat? *This* Sat? This week?

A police car cruised the street. The Policemen were young and fair-haired. They looked at Mark and smiled. Oh yes, they were Robots all right. Robots always smiled. But did they know about the pill? He walked doggedly along the pavement and the police car kept pace.

Bus Drivers smile. Assistants smile. Policemen smile. With a great effort Mark smiled back. The Officers watched him for a moment and then drove away. They had stopped smiling.

A Traffic Warden was checking the cars. Was she a Robot too? How many were there? Bus Drivers. Assistants. Police . . . How many more? Could they really tell that he hadn't taken the yellow pill? He didn't think he'd ever missed before. Just one little old pill . . . The Traffic Warden looked up from her pad and smiled. Better not to take chances. Mark forced his mouth into a smile and kept it there till she was out of sight.

The lights at the pelican crossing were against him.

He pushed the button and the standing man appeared. Red man change to green. Red man change to green . . . But the red man stared back unmoved. Mark couldn't take his eyes off him. Red man change to green. Red man . . . Red man . . . red . . . red . . .

The light began to pulse. Mark stood transfixed at the edge of the pavement. The urge to cross was strong. There was no danger . . . The traffic didn't matter . . . All that mattered was the pulsing light . . . Getting to the light . . .

A double-decker bus flashed by, breaking the contact. Janina saw Mark and waved but Mark didn't see her. As soon as he was released he ran headlong down the road. As far from the crossing light as possible.

Where was he going? He didn't care. Down the road. Round the corner. Across the street. Which street? It didn't matter. Run . . . run . . . keep going . . .

No. People are watching. Slow down. Walk. Left, right, nice and steady. Left, right, nice and steady . . .

The streets were long and unfamiliar. No bus stops. No bus route. The shops were shut and only a few people walked there. Mark began to feel very vulnerable. He wasn't sure which way he should go – and he didn't dare stop and ask. He plodded on. Right foot . . . right foot . . . The sound echoed in the empty street.

An alley-way opened in the wall to his left. It was long and narrow but there were bright lights at the far end. Mark turned and ran as fast as he could between the high walls.

Chapter Five

But panic had sent Mark round in a circle. Right back to the shopping centre. He could make out the names of the shops as he came nearer. Smith's. Dixons. Miss Selfridge.

He stopped running and stared across Western Road. Everything seemed perfectly normal. The front plaza was crowded. The lights were all on. And there wasn't a Policeman or a Traffic Warden in sight. A perfectly normal Sat afternoon . . . but for some reason he felt safer between the high walls of the alley. He melted back into the side entrance of Marks and Spencer.

What now? Walking home hadn't been much of a success. Perhaps he could risk a bus? He peered up at the Telecom clock. Twenty past three. There were lots of buses. Lots of people milling about the bus shelters. He could wait till he saw a fourteen, rush across at the last minute, squeeze on with the crowd and sit at the back. Only a ten-minute bus ride and then home. Home! With any luck the house would be empty and he could sit quietly with Monk and think things out. And if it wasn't? Mark sighed. He didn't like lying to the Mother. He always had the feeling that she knew. No good saying he didn't feel well. Martin hadn't turned up? He'd spent all his money? He sighed again. He hadn't even bought a magazine.

A bunch of girls flushed him out of the doorway and he followed them as far as the toy shop and pretended to be examining the display of electric trains. In the plate-glass window the lights of the square were reflected like a string of beads. Cluster. Single. Cluster. He turned to look at them. There was no need for artificial light. The third sun had risen. The second hadn't quite set. Between them the mirror-glass windows of the Telecom Tower scattered light in all directions.

Mark shivered. There was something eerie about the tower. It stood in front of the square and a little to one side. Massive pillar-legs raised its shining body above the hurly-burly of every day and under it, right under the yawning cavern, was a circle of tiles. Strange tiles to find in a modern shopping centre. The glaze was all cracked and burnt, but he knew from his school project that underneath there were images of a knight's helmet and a fish and a star. His class were doing 'Brighton at War' and he'd seen photographs of the bomb damage. Even pasted pictures of the tiles in his book. This was all that was left of the old town hall. A circle of dirty old tiles with cracked glaze. Not bright and shiny like the Telecom Tower with its revolving turret and its one enormous unblinking clock-face eye.

A number fourteen bus squealed to a stop. Mark nipped through the traffic and joined the queue behind a fat woman with a dozen shopping bags.

'Hello, Mrs Andrews. Hello, Mrs Smith . . .' The Driver greeted everyone as he handed out the tickets. 'Hello, Peter. Had a good day? On your way home, are you, Mrs Thomas?'

The fat lady's bags were on the step. Mark moved up behind her. Nearly there now. Only five minutes and . . .

'Well, Mrs Grieg. What have you got there? All of Boots and half of Tesco's I shouldn't wonder!'

Mrs Grieg laughed and her body shook as she heaved herself on to the bus. Mark took hold of the hand rail and stood with one foot poised. Almost home. Almost there. And then he remembered about the pill. What if the Driver knew too?

He let his hand slide off the rail and an old man pushed him aside and got on the bus.

'Well, good day to you, Mr Willis! Been to town, have you?'

Mr Willis murmured somthing, the ticket machine clicked and the Driver leaned towards the open door.

'Any more for any more?'

A woman in the queue shouted back and he laughed and drove off. Mark was left standing irresolutely by the bus shelter.

'You should have shouted!' The woman nudged him. 'Going home are you? There won't be another fourteen for twenty minutes.'

Mark muttered something and moved away. The last thing he wanted was mothering.

A smell of new bread made his nostrils twitch and reminded him of the pudding he hadn't eaten. Was there a Hot Bread Shop among the shopping precincts? There might be. There must be! He would have a doughnut. Just one doughnut – and a cake to take home to the Mother. That would please her! He skirted the front parade of shops and went into Churchill Square.

It was still crowded. Young couples shopping. Mothers with their bags. Fathers with their parcels. Babies. Students. Old people. Young people. Friends meeting. Friends parting. Everyone in a good humour and going about their business. They swept Mark along with them as they poured from one group of shops to another. Surging in and out of open doorways. Calling to each other. Laughing. Chattering. The sound of their voices was as reassuring as the smell of fresh bread that led him on.

Further into the square. Past the first concourse. Past the entrance to the underground car park. Through the colonnades. Round by the escalators. Past Habitat. Past Mothercare. Past Sainsbury's. Deeper into the square. Mark stopped. The fresh bread smell had disappeared. He turned towards Western Road again.

But now he had to face the people – and they no longer smiled. Their eyes were hard as they crossed from store to store. With arms linked and bodies close together it was impossible to get between them. Oncoming crowds with gift-wrapped plants and shopping bags drove him relentlessly back. Men pushed lines of trolleys into his path. Old ladies hauled their carts against his legs. No matter which way he turned, the way to the front of the square was barred.

For a while Mark struggled, battling against the tide of human bodies, but there was no escape. Giving up, he turned and was swept along in the crush. Past the Solarium. Past the Gas Showrooms. Along the row of insurance offices. Through the passage with the mock-Tudor antique shops . . .

And then he was being pressed against a low wall. The crowd had split into two streams and was flowing right and left around a sunken garden. Mark leaned over the parapet. Rock gardens. Lily ponds. A fountain. But no people. The garden was deserted. He clambered on to the pediment and jumped down. He threw himself on to one of the wooden benches and lay there with his chest heaving painfully and the blood pounding in his ears. He half-expected to be followed – but no one else came into the garden. No one else had even noticed him. They were all laughing and chatting again. All very friendly and pleasant. All the same, he was trapped.

His breath began to come easier and his heart stopped racing. He sat up and looked around. The water garden was a dismal place. A block of fretted stone loomed over the pools. *The Spirit of Brighton* it said on the plinth but it was far too gloomy for Brighton. No wonder people ignored it. No wonder it was deserted.

Some children leaned over and looked down on him. No. Not at him. They were laughing at something on the other side of the fountain. And gradually Mark became aware of a new sound. A sort of clang-bang. More people stopped to look. Clash-bang-honk. Clash-bang-honk-honk. Jang-bang-crash-bang. Was it a trick? He stood up, ready to make a run for it. Clash-bang-jang-bang. Clash-bang-jang-bang. A one-man band came strutting round the lily ponds.

With every movement he made one of his instruments play. The drum on his back. The squeeze-box in his hands. The mouth-organ on its wire. The horn on the brightly painted ARP helmet he wore for a hat. Jang-bang-crash-bang-honk-honk. And with every step of his red-trainered feet, the cymbals on his knees clashed and the bells round his ankles rang. Jog-trot-jang-bang . . . Jog-trot-jang-bang.

People pressed against the wall. They leaned over. They smiled. Some even threw pennies. 'Col and Zip' it said on the drum. Col – that must be the man – but who, or what, was Zip? Mark looked around but there was no one else in the garden.

And then he saw it. A monkey. Perched on the man's shoulders. At first he thought it was a toy like Monk. It had the same crooked smile. The same sad face. But there were two eyes staring out at the crowd. Two boot-black eyes that searched and searched until they met Mark's own.

A penny rattled on the paving stones. The monkey scampered down and snatched it up. Clash-bang-jang-bang. In the blink of an eye it had caught up with Col and leapt on to his shoulder again. Clash-bang-jang-bang . . . Around the dismal gardens they went. The man and his monkey. And the sound and the strange rhythm seemed to weave a spell of safety around the fountains.

Suddenly the music stopped. Col straightened up to listen. Above the dull roar of the square Mark could hear it too. The high-pitched whine of a police siren coming along Western Road. Louder . . . Closer . . .

Mark looked desperately for a way out. A way of escape. But the garden was still hemmed about with people. Col hunched over and started to play again. Clash-bang-jang-bang . . . He came between the pools. Jog-trotting right up to Mark. Looking at him with strange grey eyes. Deep into Mark's heart he looked until Mark could bear it no longer.

'Please . . .' he whispered. 'Please!'

And the man smiled. 'Follow me!' he said.

Mark followed. Taking hold of the old coat-tail he tried to keep close to the jolting figure as it danced among the fountains. Step-hop-step-hop. Unless he copied it exactly the cloth jerked out of his hand. Jog-trot-step-hop. The noise of the drum reverberated through his whole body but he hardly noticed. Clash-bang-jang-bang. Jog-trot-step-hop. At last he got it. Jog-trot-step-hop. Jog-trot-step-hop. Round the flower-beds they went one last time. Past the dripping stone and up the steps. The people heard the drum and stepped aside, smiling as the strange procession passed. The man . . . and his monkey . . . and his boy. Some of them tossed coins but now Zip had no time for money. Clinging to the painted helmet he sat upright, his eyes alert as they scanned the way ahead.

Out in the road a black van screeched to a halt. Policemen rushed into the crowds. Searching. Searching. Working their way through the precincts to the wall of shops at the back of the square.

Mark lost all sense of time and place. He danced after Col, twisting and turning and hopping and jog-trotting round and back, going this way and that as the monkey guided them. The one sure and certain thing was the coat-tail in his hand and he clung on to it for dear life.

Round and through and forwards and backwards they danced. Circling the groups of shoppers. Dodging the line of blue uniforms that advanced amongst them. The drum boomed in Mark's ears and the faces became a blur as they flew past. Faster . . . Faster . . . Out to the freedom of the street.

But there at the kerb the police car waited. Mark would have followed, trusting, if the man had led him past it. But no. He swung away again and, using the shoppers as a screen, made his way across the front plaza. Dodging and dancing and hooting and banging and all the time weaving along the margin of the crowd till they gained the sanctuary of the Telecom Tower.

It was quiet there. Col had stopped dancing and the band was still. Mark stumbled towards one of the pillars and pressed his brow against the welcome cold of the concrete. The drum-beats went on echoing in his head and he shut his eyes and waited for the sound to die away.

When he looked up again he was alone.

Frantically he rushed out into the wide front plaza. Scanned Western Road. Nothing. Neither man nor monkey. Panic mounted inside him and gathered into a sob. How had they disappeared so quickly? Where had they gone? He rushed back under the tower. Nothing. The tiles were criss-crossed with shadows as the second and third suns greeted each other across the sky but of the man and his monkey there was no trace.

Mark stood in the very centre of the circle. Trying to think. Trying to work it out. But his brain wasn't working any more. Clash-bang-jang-bang . . . Step-hop . . . Suddenly he felt very, very tired. Too tired to stop the great sobs that shuddered through him. Had it all been a dream? A nightmare? Just one more part of a very strange day? How could he tell? How could he tell anything any more? Tears rolled down his cheeks as he scuffed his foot against the roughness of the tiles. The film show. The traffic lights. Being trapped in the square. Had he imagined it all? But the man and his monkey had been real. Surely they had been real? If only he could be sure.

He kicked the tiles again – harder this time so that he felt the pain in his toes – and something shot across the circle and bounced off one of the pillars. Something shiny. He wiped his eyes and dropped to his knees. The grouting between the tiles had burnt out and something was glinting from one of the cracks. He hooked it out with his finger and held it up to the light. It was a little brass bell.

Now he was sure.

Chapter Six

Sun. Mark lay very still in the bed. Thinking. Trying to make sense of the day before. Surely he'd imagined it all? The music? The crossing light? *The Pink Panther*? Being trapped in the square? He shuddered as he thought about the crowds in the shopping precinct.

If Janina hadn't taken the headphones from him. If the bus hadn't passed. If Col hadn't rescued him . . . If he hadn't dropped the pill? It was all very confusing and questions didn't lead to answers. They led to more questions.

Col and Zip and the bell . . . If only Monk had two bright eyes and shining fur and a quivering tail. If only Monk had been able to jump on his shoulder when he called! He poked the button eye back into its socket. Was there a glint of intelligence there? But the button dropped out again and hung on its length of red thread. Only a button and some thread. He sighed. Perhaps the Father was right. Perhaps it was time the old thing went to Oxfam. He ran one finger along the lumpy

44

scar. 'Monk is mended'. How did he know that? There was something deep in his mind. Something he almost remembered. Monk was part of it but he wasn't sure how. No. He'd never give Monk away. Maybe he was just a toy – but he was special all the same. And just holding him made all the strangeness of yesterday more bearable.

He pushed back the cover and tried to get out of bed without making it move. That was another thing. The bed was as steady as a rock during the day but it could be set swinging by the slightest motion when he first woke up. And the Mother always knew. Sure enough, in she came.

'Good morning, Mark. Did you sleep well?'

'Yes, thank you.' Mark sat up and held out his hand. The Mother tipped the pill out of the paper cup and passed him the orange juice.

He looked at the smooth yellow capsule nestling in his palm. Well? He picked Monk up again. Well? He raised his hand to his mouth and made a great deal of noise about swallowing the juice. The Mother stood waiting. When he had finished she smiled and squashed the paper cup.

'Is it school today?' Mark handed back the tumbler.

'No. No school today. Today is Sun. Football today.'

'Can I be green?'

'Yes Mark, you can be green.' She fetched a green strip and shorts and laid them on the bed. 'Where are your jeans?'

'Jeans?'

'The ones you wore yesterday.'

'I . . . I bunged them in the wardrobe.'

'Mark! When will you ever learn? Dirty clothes go in the basket!'

Mark bit his lip as he watched her bring out the jeans. Would she be angry? He hadn't been very clever. She would see the burnt patch. Would she know what caused it? Oh, why had he opened the capsule? The denim had been perfectly all right before the silver powder touched it. Strong. Blue. Threads neatly woven together.

'They'll do for today,' she said, looking them over. 'You'd best get up.'

As soon as the door had clicked behind her Mark sprang out of bed and lifted the trousers to the light.

'There isn't a spot on them!'

Monk stared, unmoved.

Mark felt the material. Smelt it. Scratched it with his fingernail . . . 'Nothing to show where the powder burnt into it! But it did . . . didn't it?'

Still Monk stared.

'That pill can't be harmless! It can't be!' He felt in his

46

pocket for the yellow capsule. 'That silver and blue powder really did burn! And not taking it really did make yesterday different!'

He sat down again. Yesterday. Yesterday had been all the time like the early mornings when his mind was free. When he knew there was something wrong. But what? Everything was there. Everything had been in place. Father. Mother. White room. Brighton. The Pier. The Pavilion. The cinema. The sea. So why this feeling that it wasn't quite right? And why did no one else notice it? Martin had enjoyed the crisps. Janina had heard the music. None of them questioned anything. Phil didn't even know what his Father made. Mark frowned. He wasn't sure what his own Father did. Hadn't he ever asked? He supposed he must have but he couldn't remember getting any answer. It hadn't seemed important till now.

Round and round and round . . .

'Why couldn't I see out the back of Martin's house? Why was his Mother so aggressive?' He picked up Monk again. 'Do you suppose Martin takes a pill every morning? He's never mentioned it. Perhaps everyone takes pills. Perhaps it's just part of the routine like washing and brushing your teeth. No one ever talks about boring things like that!'

He rubbed the capsule between his fingers,

careful not to let it come apart.

Well? Would he or wouldn't he? He cuddled Monk again. What did the yellow capsule do? What would happen if he didn't take any more?

He drew the bell carefully from under his pillow and examined it. No pattern around it. Nothing special about it. Just an ordinary brass bell from the ankle-strap of a one-man band . . .

But if that was real – then so was Col. He rolled it gently around the palm of his hand. It made an odd, discordant sound that reminded him of something. Something from long ago. Long ago . . .

The words still teased his brain. Something he almost remembered. But there was a shadow in front of it. Like a curtain, only he couldn't draw it aside. Not deliberately. Sometimes it would tremble as if it was about to lift and then . . .

He gave Monk a squeeze. 'How would I know anything was wrong if I didn't have you?' he whispered. 'If only you could help me to remember . . .' But remember what?

'Mark!' It was the Mother again. 'Don't you want any breakfast?'

'Coming!' He jumped up. Of course everyone must take pills. All he had to do was ask! He wrapped the bell in a tissue and put it into the hiding-place with the pill.

Football today. He pulled on his clothes. He would ask Martin. No need to say why. Martin wouldn't want to know anyway. Clever — but not curious. That was Martin. Yes. He'd ask him today.

The Father was eating breakfast. The Mother fiddled with the toaster. Cornflakes in the bowl. Three pieces of toast in the rack. Coffee bubbling in the pot.

The Father put down his paper. 'And what is it today?'

'Football.' Mark sloshed some milk into his bowl.

'Football, eh? Do you score many goals?'

Mark mumbled an answer.

'Don't speak with your mouth full,' said the Mother.

'Goals, eh?' said the Father. 'One of these days I'll have to come and see you.'

Out in the playing field Martin was waiting. Martin was green as well and they played together and fought for the ball and every now and then Ref came and played too. Ref didn't kick the ball. He just blew his whistle and pointed. They raced from one end of the smooth green field to the other, passing the ball between them. Phil was there too but he was playing with David. The Spurling twins played together and Trevor played with Mick. They all chased separate footballs and Ref ran amongst them whistling and pointing.

Martin was dribbling the ball in a wide circle. 'Come on! Take it off me!'

Mark ran alongside. 'This is stupid,' he said.

'What's stupid?'

'Why do we kick this ball?'

Martin looked up in amazement. 'It's Sun! We play football! No school!'

'Come on – play!'

Ref ran up to them, blowing his whistle. And suddenly Mark knew as sure as anything that Ref was a Robot too.

He took the ball off Martin and kicked it up to the other end of the field.

'Come on! Run!' Ref put his whistle away and stopped to talk to David.

'Do you want a goal?' puffed Martin.

'No. Hey – Martin – slow down a minute . . . Did you know Ref was a Robot?' Martin came to a sudden stop.

'Ref?' he said. His face was all screwed up with the effort of running. He took off his glasses and polished them on the tail of his shirt.

'This isn't really a game at all.' Mark went on.

'It's football!'

'But last week you were red and I was blue and we still played together.'

'Last week?'

'Don't you remember? *The Pink Panther . . .*?'

'What is this "last week"?'

Mark made one more effort. 'Another Sun,' he said. 'Before this one . . .'

But Martin had put his glasses on again and was starting to laugh. 'That's a good one!' he said. 'Another Sun! I must tell Ref!'

'No!' Mark lifted the ball before his friend could run off with it. 'It's OK! It's Sun! We play football!'

'You're crazy!' said Martin.

'Hand ball! Hand ball!' Ref ran up to them. 'Penalty kick!' He took the ball and placed it on the ground. Martin ran at it and kicked it into the empty goalmouth. And from all around the empty stadium came the chant of 'Goal! Goal! Goal!'

Martin looked pleased with himself and Ref patted him on the back but Mark looked round at the vacant seats and inside his head the chant turned to 'Why? Why? Why?' But now it wasn't just a feeling. Now he was quite sure that something was wrong. The game. The goals. But why only him? Why did no one else see it?

A cold hard feeling gripped his stomach. There was an answer but he didn't want it to be right. What if . . . What if the world was really the perfectly normal place everyone thought it was? What if it was he, Mark who was out of step? Not quite right in the head? What if his friends were right when they said he was crazy? Maybe the pills were to keep him from getting worse. Maybe he *was* crazy.

For a minute the stadium, the pitch, the players all became a dark blur and he felt himself swaying.

'No way!' He dropped to one knee and pretended his bootlace had come undone. 'No way! They're not carting me off!'

'Goal! Goal! Goal!'

The sound echoed round and round him. It was impossible to shut it out.

'Goal! Goal! Goal . . .'

His eyes began to focus again. Ref was running towards him. He could see the glinting whistle and the pointing finger . . .

He made one mighty effort. 'Goal! Goal! Goal!' he shouted. 'Goal! Goal! Goal!'

And the black and white figure looked at him and smiled. 'Play!' he said.

Chapter Seven

'Great game!'

'I scored three goals!'

'I'm whacked!'

'Same here. Great game though!'

'Yeah. Great game!'

Mark listened to his friends as they rubbed themselves down in the showers. They were all like Martin. All happy and pleased with themselves.

Long rows of droplets made an arc towards him. He shivered as the cold water hit his body. That felt real enough. And the floor under his feet. And the taste of chlorine in the water. And the brown rivulets of mud running down his shins. He watched as they lurched from one bead of clear water to the next until they fell to the floor and were sucked through the bars of the drain. There was something terribly familiar about it – and yet it was all entirely wrong.

Everything was wrong. The green tiles on the wall. Perfect. The row of showerheads. Perfect. The sunlight pouring in through the south window – and the north. Why was everything so clean? Why was everywhere so light? So new? Even the mud looked more like paint than dirt. Why was everyone else so complacent about it? Well. Time to find out about the pills.

He shook himself and stepped out. 'Hey Phil!' he called, trying to sound casual. 'Had your pill this morning?'

There was silence as the other boys stared at him.

'What's the matter? Can't you swallow your little yellow pill, then?' jeered Trevor.

'Of course I've had it!' said Phil. 'What's got into you?' He aimed a long stream of water across the floor and they all laughed as Mark lifted his towel and ran to the changing room.

So he wasn't the only one who took the pills! That was a relief. If the pills were to stop people from going crazy then he wasn't alone.

'All going round the bend together!' he mumbled happily as he rubbed himself. Then he stopped. That didn't really solve the problem. The towel moved more slowly as he contemplated a world where everyone was mad. It didn't seem very likely. He didn't feel the least bit mad himself. All the strange things really had happened, he was sure of that. He couldn't prove most of them – but he had the bell. If Col and Zip were real then so was all the rest. He just wished he could remember . . .

The towel stopped moving altogether. Remember! But of course! That was what the pills were for! To stop them remembering! Poor Martin! 'Last week? What is this last week?' No wonder he didn't question the goals or the Ref or the film show! They couldn't remember yesterday, far less last week! No last week . . . No last year? Where had he been last year?

'Not here, that's for sure!' Mark pulled his clothes over his still-damp body. The other boys had drifted into the changing room. Should he say something? What? 'You've got to stop taking the pills'? 'Something funny's going on'? No good. They'd just look blank. No one would believe him . . . Not unless he could prove it . . .

'But something *is* going on – and I'm not taking any more of these precious pills till I find out what it is.'

Martin was still shivering in his towel. Funny how vulnerable he looked without his glasses. Mark stared at the pink eyes and the wobbling flesh.

No. Martin didn't know everything. He'd been suckered like the rest. He'd take some convincing too. He didn't like not being in the know. Still. Perhaps if Mark showed him the bell . . . And once Martin was convinced . . .

Mark pulled on his clothes and went over.

'Look. I've got something important to tell you,' he said. 'Come over to my house this afternoon.'

'I can't.' Martin stood on one foot and rubbed the other against the back of his leg.

'OK. I'll come to yours.'

Martin changed feet and pulled the towel tighter. 'No . . . I can't. I'm busy,' he said, looking down at the floor.

'But we . . .'

Mark was going to say, 'But we always do something together on Sun' but he changed his mind and asked what was the matter instead.

Martin shuffled about and picked at a long thread of cotton that dangled from the edge of his towel.

'It's the Mother,' he said at last. 'She . . . Well . . . She wants me to help her this afternoon.'

He didn't look up and Mark knew it was a lie.

'All right,' he said, keeping his voice even. 'I'll see you at school then.' And he rammed the muddy boots into his bag and strode off.

So that was it! The Mother! He'd been right. She didn't like him! Well, he didn't like her much either!

He left the Pavilion and started back across the park, kicking anything that got in his way. Her eyes were small and mean. She hadn't wanted him to see what was at the back of the house. Now she'd even turned Martin against him.

'Mean and piggy-eyed.' He aimed a particularly vicious kick at a tuft of grass. 'No good trying to save Martin. She'd probably know in an instant if he didn't take his pills. She probably knows everything anyway. She's probably a Robot!'

Mark laughed as he said it – and then a cold feeling started in the damp hair at the back of his neck. If *she* was a Robot then . . .? For a moment he stood stock-still as icy fingers spread the prickles over his scalp. If Martin's Mother . . .

Suddenly he realized that his body had taken flight. He was running. Flying . . . Escaping from the harsh empty space in the middle of the park. But the legs didn't seem to belong to him. The feet – he felt them hit the turf . . . crunch on the gravel . . . sink into the soft earth of the flower-beds – but they seemed a million miles away and he had lost control.

Rose bushes seized at him, catching at his clothes, scratching his hands. Soft green laurels barred his way. Spiky twigs tangled with his hair as he pushed into the deepest part of the shrubbery. A strand of bramble snared his ankles and sent him crashing to the ground. His elbow struck a rock. Thorns whipped across his face but he hardly noticed them. He lay there, conscious only of the one fact he was running away from. The Mother was a . . . No. He still couldn't say it.

He screwed his fists against his eyes and tried to block out the pain – but it was no use. The silent screams beat round the inside of his skull. Wave after wave of them went juddering through him, shouting out the one word he didn't want to hear. 'Robot . . . Robot . . . Robot . . .'

He might have lain there for ever if he hadn't heard the sound of laughter. He had forgotten the Gardeners' hut. Two of them were wheeling their barrows towards it now. Coming to collect their sandwiches and brew up some tea. He could hear the trundle of iron wheels and the low murmur of voices coming closer.

Mark held his breath. Children weren't allowed to play around the hut.

He sat up carefully and wiped his eyes. He no longer wanted to know what was happening. All he wanted now was to get back home. To rescue the yellow pill from its hiding place and swallow it. Who cared if this was real? Who cared what was happening? All he wanted was to swallow the pill and escape into the happy complacency of a world without memory. To make everything as it had been before. Before he had dropped the capsule. Before he had started thinking.

He wasn't making much sense but it didn't matter. Nothing mattered except getting home.

He waited till a thin wisp of smoke rose from the Gardeners' hut. They had stoked up their fire. They'd be sitting, eating, waiting for the kettle to boil. With any luck they would be there for a good hour. An hour for lunch. Even Robots must have an hour for lunch . . .

But the joke wasn't even funny. Quickly he disentangled himself from the bramble bush, ripping his sleeve some more as he tore himself loose. Home. Get home. He picked his way back through the trees, squeezed between the protective clumps of laurel and stumbled out into the rose garden. Then he ran.

The Mother was waiting for him.

'Mark! Whatever have you done to yourself? Have you been fighting?' Her scolding followed him upstairs. He banged his bedroom door and ran to the secret hiding place. The pill was still in the first aid box. Goodbye last week. Goodbye yesterday . . .

But Monk was looking at him. There was something appealing about his crooked face. Mark jumped up.

'No!' he shouted and threw the toy savagely to the top of the wardrobe.

His mouth was dry and the pill stuck in his throat.

He rushed to the bathroom and swallowed glassful after glassful of water.

'Are you all right, Mark?' The Father rattled the door.

'I'm OK!'

To his surprise his voice sounded quite calm.

'Be quick then. We're waiting lunch for you.'

The Father's footsteps faded down the stairs and Mark sat on the edge of the bath and waited for the pill to take effect.

Nothing happened. The dolphins played happily over the plastic shower curtain. The water made the same old gurgling sound. The tiles remained steadily geometric.

He got up and washed his face and from the mirror in the medicine cabinet his own grey eyes stared back at him.

After a while he turned off the taps and ran downstairs.

Chapter Eight

Mon . . . Tues . . . Wed . . . Thurs . . . The days went by in perfect unquestioned order. Mark no longer wanted a quiet time to think. As soon as he woke up he shook the bed and there was the Mother with the pill and orange juice. No time to think. No need. He only had to swallow and the world was real.

Mon. Tues. Wed. Thurs . . . He washed, dressed, ate and went to school. His class was still doing 'Brighton at War' and he pasted old photographs into his folder and wrote neat captions for them. *Coastal Defence Batteries in Lewis Crescent. Army Blows Gaps in Piers. Troops Billeted in Aquarium. Cellars of Royal Pavilion Strengthened. Air Raid Shelters in Parks. The Town Hall Before the Bombing.* None of it meant anything. It was just something to do.

He came home, watched TV, did his homework and went to bed again. Within seconds he had fallen willingly into a deep sleep where there were no dreams. He didn't remember exactly what had happened at the weekend. He only knew it had been dangerous and unpleasant and that he didn't ever want to go through it again. Not even to think about it.

Mon . . . Tues . . . Wed . . . Thurs. The School Bus Driver smiled pleasantly at him. The Keeper made jokes as he crossed the park. No pulsing red man called him into the flow of traffic. No patrol car cruised beside him as he walked along. He swallowed his pill like a good boy and everything went back to normal. Mark went to school. The Father went to work. The Mother stayed at home.

Thursday was the Mother's cleaning day. She was very thorough. She found Monk on top of the wardrobe and put him back on his usual perch – clinging to the white padded headboard of Mark's bed.

Mark had cricket practice and was late home. He ate supper and watched TV for a bit, but it was boring and he was glad to go upstairs. He threw his cricket gear on the floor, undressed and got into bed. He didn't notice Monk. As soon as his head hit the pillow his eyes shut tight against the brightness of the fourth sun and he lay there, waiting for the hazy warmth that was the harbinger of sleep.

But no sleep came. The quiet noises of the house still tied him to the waking day. He heard the music for the late evening news. The Father moving about in the sitting room. The Mother making a last cup of tea. And a jumble of sounds that could have been from the TV – or from outside – or maybe were only in his head. He thought he was awake but his heavy eyes refused to open.

He tossed and turned, trying to find some way down into the comfort of oblivion but it was no good. He was stuck somewhere between sleeping and waking and could find no peace.

The late-night buses rumbled into town. A motorbike roared past, its throttle open, its engine screaming to the sky. The whine of it hung on the air until the bike was long gone and Mark was no longer sure whether he could actually hear it or not.

At last there was the quiet tread of Parents coming up the stairs. The sound of water running in the cistern. The click of the pull switch and the soft thud of the bedroom door. At last the house was still. Surely now sleep would come? He gave a mighty heave and settled on his left side.

And in the white room the bed shook and Monk slipped forward and leaned too far and toppled down on to the pillow. And almost at once a dull warmth made Mark's body glow and he felt himself melting into darkness. Into a dark and endless ocean.

But the darkness was not absolute. Shadows flickered

through it. Great grey shadows that circled round him. Nearer and nearer until they were almost touching. He stretched out his arms and felt the strong, warm bodies. Dolphins! But these were not the plump, stylized creatures that twined around the Brighton lamp posts. Nor the funny cartoon fish of the shower curtains. These were great and strange and wonderful and had the power to banish fear. And they were swimming closer to him . . . closer . . . until he understood that they wanted him to swim with them . . . leap with them . . .

He sat astride a great grey back and the gentle beast took him down . . . down . . . down into the depths. Then the great tail flicked and he had to cling on to the dorsal fin as they turned towards the light. The water flowed past him in a silver stream. Up . . . Up . . . Bubbles tickled his nose and clung to his hair . . . and shook free as they broke the surface of the water.

High into the air they sprang, arching through the sky. And the drops of water turned into a million stars. Mark held his breath. No need to hold on. He and the dolphin were as one. Flying. Flying through the moonlit sky. No need to blink. This was a pale half-light that didn't hurt his eyes. A dark sky pierced with stars. A luminous ocean.

Only now it was all fading. There were no stars. No dolphins. From far away his feet felt wet and he shivered as his body trembled into life.

He was standing in a familiar garden. Rose bushes leaned with the prevailing wind and the grass was laden with crystals of dew. His bare feet felt cold against them and the chill spread through his body.

He shivered. Had he been sleep-walking?

A cloud crossed the face of the moon and the garden drowned in night. He stood where he was, afraid to go forward without light. Then, as his eyes got used to the glim, he saw the stand of pampas-grass quivering in the cool night air, its banners shining silver, its slender stalks merging with the purple shadows of the earth. The moon alternately hid and revealed herself but Mark was no longer afraid. He felt akin to this silver world of the moon and the shadows and he wanted it to last for ever.

Inside his own house he climbed the stairs to bed again. The moonbeams cast strange patterns on the walls. There was no red. No yellow. No green. Purple and blue and silver were the colours of the moon and everything was quiet and still and waiting.

His bedroom was just as he had left it. White wardrobe. White chest of drawers. The pile of white cricket gear beside the chair. Why then did it feel different? It was all his – so why did he feel an intruder here?

A small tight knot of fear gathered in his stomach. Gathered and spread so that he could hardly breathe. The bed . . . why was the cover humped up like that? Why did it move as if a restless body lay beneath?

He took a step nearer . . . and the cover heaved and an arm stretched out along the pillow and a fair head turned and turned and Mark felt the world turning as he looked down on his own sleeping face.

The scream seemed to come from deep inside him and he was running. Screaming. Stumbling blindly along the corridor towards his parents' room.

His father woke – white-faced, alarmed. His mother sat up – blinking and wide-eyed from sleep. Soft arms reached out and folded round him and he pressed his face deep into the damp warmth of flesh and skin until the screaming stopped.

'All right . . . It's all right now . . .' They said it over and over, crooning tunelessly as they swayed and rocked, the three of them together.

'All right . . . All right now . . .'

Love wove defences round him with their arms. His eyes were heavy and he felt his eyelids drop. The crooning sound went on as darkness ebbed and flowed and carried him away. He felt himself sinking . . . sinking . . . until his feet touched bottom and he woke to find himself in his own white bed again.

Chapter Nine

Mark stared up at the ceiling, hardly knowing what had happened. Was he Mark? Was this his own room? He lay still, listening to the harshness of his breath and trying to reorientate himself to the world of the four suns.

Everything seemed to be in place. White walls. White curtains. White chest of drawers. White lampshade. White table. White chair. Even the discarded cricket gear. Everything in order. White. Shining. New. He was Mark and he was in his own room. Last night had only been a dream. Gradually he allowed himself to relax and the sound of his breathing became quiet and even.

And then the image of the figure in that other moon-pale bed flashed into his mind and the taste of fear made his tongue stick dry to the top of his mouth and his insides turned back to jelly. Did you see yourself in dreams? In nightmares? No. His nightmares were usually about crawling things. Centipedes and spiders . . .

So who was he, the boy in the bed? He'd seemed so

real . . . But there couldn't be two Marks! Could there? He swallowed hard. Was it possible that it was he, himself, who was the dream?

Gingerly he flexed his toes until the nails caught. Moved his fingers. Clenched and stretched them. Felt them to be part of himself. Rubbed them slowly up his arms . . . On the left elbow was the scar where the rocks had drawn blood. No. He was real all right. The real Mark. The genuine article. Last night had only been a dream. A different kind of nightmare. So why wasn't he bouncing up in bed and signalling that he was ready for another pill?

Part of him longed for the peace the pill would bring. The freedom from doubt. The certainty that everything was right with the world. But deeper still inside his mind, another part was awake. It did not speak with words. There were no clever arguments. But it was strong and sure and it told him as clearly as if a voice was speaking that something was wrong and that he should lie still.

He had tried to ignore that voice. Tried to escape from it by taking the pills again. But it was still there. More potent now. Demanding. Forcing him to acknowledge it.

His limbs ached with the effort to control them. He wished he hadn't thrown Monk to the top of the wardrobe. He felt lonely and vulnerable, lying motionless on the bed and not knowing what he should do. Monk would have been something familiar. Something to hold on to. Something to help him think.

He bit his lip. Maybe, if he was careful, he could retrieve the old toy without swinging the bed. Or should he just let it swing and have done with it? Shut out that inner voice. Call the Mother. Take the pill . . .

Cramp was making his legs feel hollow. He shifted position slightly and something soft tickled his ear. At first he ignored it but the tickle became more persistent. Carefully, inch by inch, he turned his head – and a blur of warm fur fell across his face.

'Monk!' he whispered. 'But how?' But it didn't matter how. Gently, very gently, he reached out a hand and drew Monk to him.

'You silly old thing! Silly old toy! Was it you that . . .?'

No. Stupid to think that an old toy monkey could have had anything to do with the dream. All the same. He felt safer now. A wave of happiness broke the tension. Now he could think clearly. And almost before he was conscious of it, the decision had been made. He would take no more pills. If he was ever to find out what was happening then the truth, however dreadful, would have to be faced. He shuddered as he remembered his flight through the park.

But now he had Monk. He clung on to the shabby toy and, no longer afraid, put the unthinkable into words.

'She *is* a Robot, isn't she?' he whispered. 'The Mother?' He held Monk closer. 'And the Father?' he shuddered. 'I don't understand. It's all mixed up. Last night I saw . . . I dreamt . . . At least I think it was a dream. I don't know how the dolphins came into it – but dreams don't have to be logical, do they?' He gave Monk another squeeze. 'But I'm the real Mark – aren't I?'

His voice died away. His eyes were hurting in the constant sunlight and he blinked the dryness away and thought longingly of the soft light of the dream world.

'Moon . . . Shadow . . . Home!' The word floated unbidden into his consciousness. 'Home . . . Home?' Home! Was that where Monk had been mended? These dream parents had loved and comforted him. No need for explanations. Their presence had been all the security he needed. Their love almost tangible. Even now the memory of it had the power to banish fear.

'Home . . .' He let the word linger. 'Home . . .' There were other words too. 'Mum . . .? Dad . . .?' He said them again. Out loud this time. 'Mum . . . Dad . . .?'

And suddenly, he knew.

'They weren't dream parents at all, were they?' He sat

up in one quick movement. 'They were my real parents, weren't they? My real Mum and Dad! And that other Mark, the one in the bed, he wasn't real! I'm real – so he can't be!' He almost laughed aloud with relief. 'There's been a swap! The wrong Mark in the right world and . . .'

But the bed had trembled. The Mother came into the room.

'Good morning, Mark!' she said. 'Did you sleep well?'

Mark's heart almost stopped. It was the same face. The same smile. Only when he looked into the eyes did he know that this was the Robot-Mother. The thought frightened him no longer. He smiled and held out his hand.

'Yes, thank you. Is it school today?' The routine was familiar. Easy.

'Yes, Mark. This is Fri. School today.' The Mother emptied the paper cup into his waiting palm.

'How often do I tell you to leave your things tidy!' she said crossly as she picked up the crumpled white trousers.

Mark watched her prop the bat and pads against the chair. Did his own mother get cross like that? No. Better not to think. Just stick to the routine. Just in case. He waited till the Mother turned her back before he slipped the pill under his pillow.

He felt wonderful! Exhilarated! It was difficult not to shout. He finished the orange juice in one gulp. He was real. The real Mark! And he'd found his real parents!

'Be quick now or you'll miss the bus!' The Robot-Mother brought out his school clothes and laid them on the bed. White shirt. Grey trousers. Black jacket. Black and gold striped tie. Mark watched impatiently. Would she never go? He passed back the silver tumbler and sat hugging his knees.

'It's this four-sunned world that's the nightmare, isn't it?' he whispered, as soon as the door was closed. 'This world of Robots and the pills that make you forget! And we don't belong here at all, do we? It's the wrong world!'

He caught his breath. 'The wrong world . . .' He said it again, more quietly this time, 'The wrong world . . .' and even as he whispered it for a third time, Mark knew that it was true.

Now the words came tumbling out. It was as if a flood barrier had been swept away and he was almost drowning in the rush of thoughts and doubts and fears that surged though him. 'Houses you can't see behind and factories that don't make anything and the Assistants and the Bus Drivers and Martin's Mother and the football match and . . . and the endlessly repeating days. The same old conversation at breakfast. The same old film at the cinema . . . It just goes round and round, doesn't it? It's just all so mind-bendingly meaningless! No wonder we have to take pills to stop us remembering! To stop us from seeing how stupid this all is!'

He rubbed his chin along the rough line of Monk's missing eye. 'This isn't my real home, is it?' he whispered. 'So what am I doing here? I don't remember coming. Don't remember a journey. A time when I could say "since then" . . .'

He jumped out of bed. 'I don't belong here. None of us do! We belong in that other world! I don't know how we got here – but it's not right. We should be there. Home. With our own fathers and mothers.' He threw off his pyjamas. 'That's what home means. Isn't it?' he said more slowly. 'The place where you belong?' He sat down beside Monk again. 'And that's what I felt last night! As if I belonged! And that's where I'm going! *Home*!'

He had a sudden flash of conscience. What about Martin and the others? Wouldn't they want to go home too? 'But they didn't believe me, did they? They just laughed.' He stroked Monk's tail. 'They wouldn't listen to me then. Probably wouldn't listen to me now. They'd just say I was crazy.' He jumped up again. 'But I'm not! It *is* wrong! And I'm going to find out why!'

The yellow pill rolled on to the floor. Mark kicked it under the bed. These silver-filled capsules were what bound him to this place. But what place? Not Earth, that was for sure. 'Not even a very good imitation!' he said out loud. '*Four* suns? Brighton with a sandy beach? Churchill Square with a Telecom clock? What happened to the fancy new shopping centre with the great domed roof and the lifts and things?'

He looked at his school uniform, laid so neatly on the bed. Everything was laid north to south across the cover. Did his real mother have a thing about tidiness? Did the other Mark, Mark II?

'Do you think Mark II is tidy?' He pulled on his trousers. 'Can't be. Otherwise Mum would know, wouldn't she? No good putting something perfect in my place! She'd know in an instant!' He picked up the white shirt. 'He wouldn't have to be tidy. Or clever at school. And she'd have to nag him about doing his homework and doing dishes and being late for meals and things.' He buttoned up the shirt and started on the tie. Was Mark II doing the same? 'So what's the point? What's the point of having a Robot that isn't perfect?' He pulled the tie off again. Did Mark II make such a hash of things? 'But he'd have to, wouldn't he? Otherwise everyone would know he wasn't me!'

He made another knot. Still not right. Better look in

the mirror and do it properly. 'Over and round and up and through.' Nursery school stuff. Or was it Cubs? His hands began to move more slowly. One Mark on this side . . . and one Mark on the other . . . Was that how the swap worked? Did it need him to be doing things . . . thinking things . . . at the same time?

'But how? And why? And *who*, for goodness' sake?'

Determinedly he thrust away the questions. There was only one person he could trust. Col. The man in the Square. He had been real. Mark remembered the grey eyes. He had helped. Perhaps he would help again. At the very least he might know what was happening.

He knelt down and felt for the yellow pill. 'No sense in leaving it for the Mother to find!' he said as he whipped the rug aside and prised up the loose floorboard. 'Yes! That's what I'll do! Find Col. I'm sure *he* was real.' He dropped the capsule into the hole. 'At least I'm sure the bell's real!'

The brass bell was still in the tissue. He unwrapped it and it rang gently. It sounded clear and cool and far away. Like the moonlight . . .

'Bathroom's free!'

Mark came to with a start as the Father called from the landing.

'Coming!' He jumped up and sent a chair crashing to the ground.

'Mark! Are you all right? What's going on in there?'

Mark just had time to kick the rug over the hole before the Robot-Father opened the door.

'What's going on?'

'Nearly ready!' Mark placed the chair carefully and sat on it. 'Just checking some homework!' He hoped the unnatural phrase sounded convincing.

The Robot-Father came right over to the table and picked up a folder.

' "Brighton at War", eh?' he said, flicking through the pages. 'Good show! Well – breakfast's ready. Don't want to keep the Mother waiting, do we!'

He replaced the book on the table. He didn't seem to be in any hurry to leave.

'Guess I'd better get a move on,' Mark said loudly. Why had the Father chosen this of all mornings to prowl round his room? Was he looking for something? There had been no time to fix the loose floorboard . . .

He tossed back the bedcovers and pretended to be hunting for a lost sock. Monk was flung on to the floor.

The Father bent down and picked him up.

'Wasn't this going to Oxfam?' he said, holding Monk by the end of his long tail.

Mark didn't know what to say. The Robot-Father was smiling but his eyes were cold. From his outstretched hand Monk hung helplessly, his loose black eye dangling as he swung about the room.

The Father laughed and twirled Monk round his head and aimed him at Mark. Mark ducked automatically and the toy went flying through the air and smashed against the wall. The Father cheered. Mark didn't move.

'Yes. Oxfam!' said the Father at last. 'Get washed now.' He threw a few mock punches as he ran downstairs.

Mark picked up the battered toy and stroked it. What should he do? Take Monk with him? Leave him here? 'No. No way!' he whispered.

He tried to push the black eye back into its socket. 'It's only fur . . . and fabric . . . and a boot-button eye . . .' he murmured. And yet . . .

'Just a collection of fur and fabric and stuffing sewn together.' He twisted the scarlet thread. 'Not even very well sewn . . .'

The button came away in his hand. Now what? For a long moment he held both Monk and the eye. Then he laid the eyeless toy gently on the bed and slipped the button into his trouser pocket.

'Yes. Find Col,' he said. 'Find Col. Find out what's happening. And then maybe . . . just maybe . . . I can find my way home.'

Chapter Ten

Mark set out that morning as if for school but he had no intention of going there.

'I'm on a project. A special project.' He rehearsed the words as he took the short cut across the Park.

The bowling greens were deserted. The tennis courts locked up. The place was eerie without people. No one strolling about. No one sunning themselves on the wooden benches. Mark had never seen the place so empty before and for some reason he felt more exposed here than out on the streets.

He frowned as he passed the locked changing rooms. Now he'd have to wear his school uniform all the way into town. Oh well. Too late now to change his mind. Soon school would start. Soon the register would be called. Before long the Truant Officer would drive out to the house to find out what was happening. Would the Mother get into trouble? She had looked after him and cared for him and if it hadn't been for the dream . . .

No. Col was the only real person. That's why he was

skipping school. Somehow he had to find Col again. He hurried on into the formal Town Garden. Only the Town Garden to get through, then the Scented Garden, and . . .

'Good morning, Mark! Missed the bus, have you?' A Park Keeper strode towards him with a cold smile.

Mark muttered something about being late and tried to dodge past.

'Late, eh? You'd better get along then. They don't like it when you're late.' The man turned to walk beside him.

'I'm . . . I'm on a special project.'

'Special project, eh? That's interesting. They didn't have special projects in my day.'

'No.' Mark walked faster but still the man kept pace. Round by the sundial. Past the rustic shelter. He could feel the power of the steel–grey eyes. Probing. Probing. Could they see into his mind? He stared straight ahead. So long as he didn't meet those eyes . . .

He was almost at the gate. Just the Scented Garden to get through . . .

'I've got to go now!' he said breathlessly.

He broke into a run. Along by the herb beds. Over the low hedges . . .

But even as he ran he could see that he was trapped. A huge padlock held the gates together and high railings shone along the perimeter wall.

Behind him he could feel the power of the Park Keeper. Feel himself slowing down. Feel the strength draining from his legs. Feel himself being forced to turn back.

Desperately he grabbed hold of the handrails in the Scented Garden. But it was no use. His fingers were loosening. Being dragged across the surface of the notices in Braille. Braille notices. Square . . . hard . . . little dots . . . lumps . . . lumps . . . Lumps! Monk!

'Monk is mended!' he whispered.

And suddenly a picture flashed into his mind. Something from his 'Brighton at War' project. A photograph of the park railings being loaded on to a lorry. A photograph of the low wall with only stumps of iron left. *All Gone* . . . the caption had said. *All Gone for the War Effort* . . .

And when he looked again there wasn't a railing in sight.

'Monk is mended!' He said it out loud. 'Monk is mended!' He shouted it as he ran for the low wall and cleared it in one bound.

When he looked back the man was smiling. 'Monkeys, eh? Well, you'll find no monkeys in my park!' And he stood by the empty gateposts and waved, and Mark hitched his duffle bag on to his shoulder and forced himself not to run until he was out of sight.

The roads were busier as he neared the centre of town. More people. More cars. Well, he didn't need to stick to the roads. Brighton was a maze of interconnecting passages. Alley-ways. People said you could get anywhere through the alley-ways. Black Ham Lane. Turk's Alley. The Cheeseway. Mark threaded his way between the buildings till he came to Western Road.

Still no Police about. No Traffic Wardens. All the same. No point in getting caught now. He waited to cross with a group of young Mothers. They laughed and chatted and paid no attention to him and he was able to stay with them until they reached Churchill Square and wheeled their prams into the ever-open doors of Mothercare.

At ten o'clock on a weekday morning the square was not the crowded place where he had been trapped. Mothers in brown dresses stood quietly outside supermarkets. Fathers in city suits hailed taxis. They didn't seem interested in a boy who should have been in school – but you could never tell. Best to avoid them.

He wished he'd been able to leave the jacket and tie at home. Better to change as soon as possible. Once the Truant Officer had visited the house the Robots would be hunting for him. No point in being an easy target.

He had an old sweatshirt in his duffle bag and there were plenty of litter bins around. He stood in an empty doorway and changed. With any luck he would be long gone before the bins were emptied.

He felt quite elated now. Soon he would know what was happening. Soon he would be safe. Yes. Even if Col didn't know what it was all about, at least he was real. That would be something. Someone to talk to. And once he'd got it sorted he could tell Martin and the others. Maybe even let them meet Col. They'd have to believe him then!

'Crazy! I'll show them who's crazy!' he muttered as he neared the Water Garden.

But there was no water trickling down *The Spirit of Brighton*. The fountains had been turned off and only a few children played on the stone benches. Only sparrows splashed in the brackish pools. His heart sank. Suddenly he felt very scared and very lonely and very tired. Now what? He knew that he should keep moving but he couldn't summon up the energy. He just stood there, his hands deep in his pockets, watching the children and the squabbling birds. Stupid children. Stupid sparrows. Stupid Mark! Of course there was no Col. Why would a one-man band play to a deserted square?

A snatch of rhythm drew him to the main shopping

area but it was only an old man tap-tapping a tuneless tune on a tobacco tin. He hurried into Tesco Homeware, up their escalator and out to the front of the square again. Two Policemen were standing by the bus stops. They seemed quite relaxed and friendly as they chatted to a pretty young woman with a push chair. But every time a bus stopped they would break off and stare intently at the passengers. Oh yes. They were looking for him all right. He turned quickly and went towards the Telecom Tower. Maybe Col . . .?

But even from a distance it was clear that no one was standing beneath it. No Col. No monkey.

'But that's where he was. That's where I saw him last. Perhaps if I wait − just for a little while.' He hurried towards the concrete pillars.

It was almost noon. The second sun was directly overhead, the third still hidden behind tall buildings. For a moment the tile circle was veiled in shadow. Mark dropped to his knees. He'd seen pictures of the tiles, of course. Even pasted them into his project book. 'Something to do with heraldry,' Miss Ritchie had said. And he had written the title neatly underneath his blurred photocopy . . . *The Unofficial Brighton Coat of Arms. 1854 to 1897.*

'A helmet . . . and a fish . . . and a star . . .' He

murmured the words to himself as one finger traced the patterns on the tiles.

'A helmet . . . and a fish . . . and a star . . .'

Only now there was no bright sunlight to catch the cracks and spread a concealing web. Now he could see right through the damaged glaze to the pictures underneath.

Mark stared at them. 'But it isn't anything to do with heraldry!' he whispered suddenly. 'A helmet . . . and a fish . . . and a star? Of course it isn't anything to do with heraldry!' He jumped to his feet. It was the dream! The dolphins and the stars of his dream! And the helmet was . . .

He felt in his pocket for the bell. Col wore a helmet, didn't he? It didn't have to be bright and shiny, did it? Wouldn't an old ARP helmet do?

The suns were moving and there was only a tiny arc of shadow left. He stumbled across the tiles and pressed himself into it and the bell found its voice and the soft echo passed from pillar to pillar. He held it high, trying not to let the sunlight touch it.

Above him, spiralling upwards, was a tunnel of darkness. Darkness above and a dark circle below. And his legs began to tremble and his mouth went dry as the ground tilted crazily and rushed up to meet him.

Now the darkness was complete.

Chapter Eleven

Mark's eyes were shut and he didn't want to open them. He was floating through space and he didn't want to spoil it. The air was damp and cool and rested on his eyelids like a balm. There were no suns. No Robots. Everything was peaceful and quiet and only a strange high whispering sound echoed through the stillness. Sometimes it was thick and insistent and almost like words. Sometimes it was stretched out so thin he wasn't sure if he could hear it or not. It didn't matter. Nothing mattered. The unreal world of the four suns was slipping further and further away. Only a dull pain stopped him from floating free of it altogether.

Like a kite, he strained against the ache that tethered him. His right shoulder had gone to sleep. Pins and needles were spreading through his arm and neck. Shooting down to his fingers. Tightening his scalp. In desperation he hauled his body over and a dizzying warmth flooded through him. The whispering air rushed past. He was being hauled down . . . down . . .

His shoulder was swelling and throbbing and his right ear was burning and another arm was stretched across his chest and another hand was rubbing . . . rubbing . . .

The bones of his back complained as they came in contact with something hard and his legs straightened and the heels of his trainers dragged and the rushing noise grew smaller and sharper and clearer − and he opened his eyes to find that it was the rustle of his own sleeve as it brushed against his face.

He lay motionless, gazing into the yawning arch of the tower that stretched above him. Shadows melting into shadows and as black as space. Only it wasn't space. He was still in the tile circle. And still alone.

He raised his head and looked around. He had never seen Churchill Square like this before. No people. No lights. No cars along Western Road. The shops were all closed and shuttered and the pavements bare. He tried to prop himself up on one elbow but the arm collapsed as soon as he put any weight on it. He groaned and rolled over and a tiny movement caught his eye. A small furry body was crouched beside a pillar. Two boot-black eyes glared at him from a crooked face.

A wild flicker of hope lifted his spirits. Col had been there. He had left the monkey. It was a sign. It was . . .

The click of sensible shoes brought him to his senses. A Policewoman was doing her rounds, checking the doors of the shops at the front of the square. Now he knew why the town centre was so quiet; it was night. Honest folk were at home and safely tucked up in bed. Everyone else was suspect.

The Policewoman was almost at the last shop in the row. So far she hadn't noticed him. Would she continue into the shopping precincts? Or was this the end of her beat? The glass doors of the Record Hut were loose. She rattled them, satisfying herself that they were really locked. Then she strolled past Smith's, examined the book display, tried the double doors and paused before the video games. For a minute Mark thought she was going to turn into the square but she changed direction sharply and marched straight towards the tower instead. Fear held him motionless. He was trapped.

He could see her beady eyes shining. See her lips moving. Hear the crackle of her radio. It was too late to crawl away. Her heel beats echoed as she strode under the tower. Right up to the edge of the tiles. And then they stopped. Mark looked around. Apart from the monkey he was alone and everything was quiet.

And then, just as suddenly, they started up again on the other side. And there she was, going away from him and disappearing along Western Road.

He was too astonished to move.

'She . . . she walked right through me!' he said aloud.

'Right through me, and I didn't feel a thing! I didn't hear anything. The footsteps stopped on the edge there and the next thing . . .'

Encouraged by the sound of a human voice, the monkey left the shelter of the pillar.

'Here – Zip!' Mark eased himself into a sitting position and held out his hand. 'You know me, don't you? Come on, fellow. Come to Mark. Do you know what's happening? Did Col leave you?' But the monkey sat shivering and silent.

Mark lifted him on to his lap. 'She didn't see us, did she? Walked right through us. She must have walked right through us. We didn't see her. Didn't hear anything. We were here and she wasn't. One minute she was there. And the next minute . . . I don't understand it – but we're safe in here, aren't we?' He sighed. 'I wish you could speak. I wish Col had come himself. Still. He must mean us to stay here, mustn't he? Maybe it's a sort of sanctuary. A safe place. And we'll be safe as long as we stay in the circle. Is that it?'

Zip didn't reply, but it was comforting to be holding something live and warm. The monkey was about the same size and shape as Monk – but he didn't take so kindly to being cuddled. He squirmed and scratched and Mark had to let him go.

'All right! All right! No need to get so bad tempered!

Here! Where are you going? Come back!' He jumped up but he was too late. Zip had run out of the circle.

'What did you have to . . . No! Zip! Don't go! I'm sorry. Come and be friends.'

The monkey paused and turned. Mark held out his hand and for a moment it looked as if Zip's curiosity would get the better of him. He walked slowly back under the tower, hand over hand and tail held high. Mark waited till all four paws were on the tiles before he lunged – but Zip was too quick for him. With a quiver of his long tail he sidestepped the grasping hands and ran out along the front plaza.

Now what was he supposed to do? Mark stood up and kicked angrily at the burnt tiles. Col had left the monkey. That meant he was coming back. He wouldn't be very pleased if Zip had disappeared.

'Why couldn't you stay where it was safe?' he yelled. 'Why should I get the blame?'

Zip had stopped to examine a waste bin. He sat on the yellow plastic and grinned.

'Blasted animal!'

The monkey sat and scratched himself and Mark began to think.

Zip had gone out . . . and in . . . and out of the circle. Why couldn't a boy do the same? It shouldn't take more than a second or two to catch one little monkey. They could be safely back in the Sanctuary by the time Col returned.

He looked along Western Road. No sign of the Policewoman. He took a deep breath and stepped out from under the tower.

He was just in time to see a tail disappearing into one of the huge brick flower pots. But when he parted the ferns Zip had gone.

'Dratted, stupid animal!'

Mark followed across the front plaza to another flower pot. To another litter bin. Always getting just near enough to pounce and always just missing. He knew that he should go back but he was furious that the monkey was making a fool of him.

But Zip had stopped running. Now he stood on his hind legs, jabbering and chattering. Mark held out his arms and Zip scrambled up and snuggled against his neck. Mark was too bewildered to be angry. It had been a very bewildering day. He held the monkey tight. He was tired of trying to work it all out by himself. But Martin hadn't listened to him. Neither had Phil. How could they help if they wouldn't listen?

He sat down on the nearest bench. How had he been able to lie in the circle all day without any of the Robots spotting him? And how come the Policewoman had just disappeared when she stepped into it?

'I don't understand it.' He sat stroking Zip. He had never been out in the middle of the night before. Was this what it was like? Nothing like his dream, that was for sure! No moon. The fourth sun shining brilliantly. Nobody about. Just old newspapers blowing along the pavements. All pretty tacky, really. Not even any lights!

'But there should be lights!' he told the monkey. 'I pasted a photograph into my project book, *Brighton Brightens Up Again*. Lights on everywhere. That's what I would have expected.'

And even as he looked at them, the street lamps began to glow. Red at first, then gradually shining cold and bright. Mark jumped to his feet.

'Just because I thought about it?' He tightened his hold on Zip. 'But supposing I'd remembered them coloured? Blue . . . or like Christmas, say . . .' He hadn't thought about Christmas for a long time, but now, memories of Christmas trees and Christmas lights . . .

'Wow!'

In two seconds the plaza had been transformed. Strings of shining stars stretched from building to building. Jewel colours lit up tall Christmas trees on every corner.

'And there used to be a display in the centre of the square! Moving reindeer and things. I expect that's . . .'

But Zip had had enough.

'No! Don't wriggle!' Mark gripped tighter. 'We've got to stay . . . Ouch!'

Zip screamed as he leapt for the nearest Christmas tree and Mark was left rubbing the bite on his cheek.

'All right! Run away! See if I care!'

Zip grinned at him from a tinsel star. No way of getting the stupid creature down from there. But if he could get rid of the tree? He'd created it. Just a moment ago the place had been bare and then he had thought about Christmas and the trees had appeared and the lights . . . What if he thought about them *not* being there?

'No more Christmas!' he said loudly. And almost before he had finished speaking the square was bare again and the lights had gone.

Zip, of course, was furious. One minute he had been climbing a tree; the next, he was dumped on the hard ground. He ran at Mark, screaming and scolding.

Mark caught the angry monkey in his arms.

'Shut up, can't you!' It might be the middle of the night but the Policewoman was probably not the only Robot around. 'You want a tree? A banana tree? Have a . . . No! I didn't mean . . .'

But it was too late. A tree was already sprouting from one of the flower pots. Within minutes it was twenty feet high and towering into the upper plaza. Green leaves spread a shady crown and a huge stalk of fruit dangled towards the excited monkey. Zip leapt from Mark's arms. Now he was hanging by his tail, swinging backwards and forwards and twisting round and round as he peeled a banana.

'OK? Satisfied?' Mark laughed aloud – and then he began to wonder. Could he really make things happen? Make things appear just by thinking about them? He'd made the lights come on, hadn't he? And Christmas? And even if Christmas hadn't been real – the bananas were! He looked up at Zip, munching away. So what about food for himself? It was a long time since breakfast. He hadn't even brought sandwiches. And even as he thought about them, a pack of sandwiches appeared. Bread and cheese. Not even mustard. The Mother wasn't very good at sandwiches. Surely he could do better than that? He pictured milk shakes . . . and chicken . . . and chips . . . and suddenly all of them were there. He pictured chocolate cake and ice cream . . . and the dishes appeared as if by magic.

'Maybe it *is* magic!' Mark's spirits lifted as he looked at the food. 'Maybe it's me! Maybe I can just . . . materialize things! Huh! Won't Martin be jealous! Poor old superior Martin! Having to ask me . . .'

Zip swung round again.

'Pretty good, eh? Bananas . . . chicken . . . Have a

chip!' He held out a chip but the monkey screamed and threw a banana skin at him.

'OK. So you're not impressed. But Martin would be! And Phil! Supposing I could materialize anything we wanted! Bikes and speed boats and things . . .' He sat down. 'Supposing I could show them what this place is *really* like,' he said more slowly. 'That would prove I wasn't crazy, wouldn't it?'

He tucked his feet up under him. Maybe he didn't need Col. He'd done all this without him. Maybe finding the real place wouldn't be so difficult. Just one little look. It couldn't do any harm, could it?

He folded his arms. So what did you have to do? Think of something? What? It certainly wasn't Earth. Another planet? Something so advanced . . . so far into the future . . .

He unfolded his arms again. This was more Martin's kind of thing. Martin was always going on about the future.

'But I don't want *Space Mag* stuff! I just want to see what's here! If it isn't really Brighton, then what is it?'

He made himself comfortable and thought about the place not being Brighton. Nothing changed. He clenched his teeth and frowned at the banana palm. Still no change.

'Oh, come on!' he said out loud. 'You did Christmas,

didn't you? It's a city, isn't it?' He closed his eyes. 'OK. What about tall white buildings and aerial roadways? Cars like silver bullets and . . .'

'Wow!' There was a deep throaty roar and he opened his eyes to find the whole place transformed. Skyscrapers glimmered in the sunlight. Moving walkways arched the gaps between. Bullet-like silver cars roared along super highways. It was fantastic . . . but it wasn't right!

'*Space Mag*!' he whispered with a sigh.

He blinked and tried again. Perspex domes and sunken living quarters this time – but they didn't look right either. Would he never get away from Martin's *Space Mag* pictures? He tried devastated buildings and flooded streets. Still no good. Houses like mushrooms? No. Crystal prisms?

The crystal prisms appeared and Mark sat looking at them. They might not be right, but they were pretty good. He couldn't remember anything like them in the magazine. A landscape of pyramids . . . Glass? Ice? The sun reflected off the shining surfaces and broke into a million colours. He smiled. He felt quite proud of them.

'Wonder if any of them are hollow?' He stood up. It would be fun to go wandering. Exploring a crystal world . . .

'No!' he said severely. This was no time for flights of

fancy. 'Just stick to the original plan. Find Col. Find out what's happening.'

He sat down again. Time to switch back to the fake Brighton. Time to find Zip. Not that he was very keen. The monkey had been nothing but trouble and the bite on his cheek was still stinging. Still. Col wasn't going to help if he'd gone and lost Zip.

'Back to Brighton!' he said cheerfully.

But nothing happened.

'Brighton!' he said again.

Still nothing.

'Zip!' he called in panic.

But the prisms went on shining and of the monkey there was no sign.

He clenched his fists. This wasn't as easy as he thought. But Christmas had disappeared, hadn't it? He'd conjured up Christmas – and then he'd got rid of it again, hadn't he? Maybe if he closed his eyes . . .

'All this stuff . . . everything that isn't real . . .' he said, 'I want it to go away.'

Well, this was no time for half measures.

'All of it!' he said firmly.

And when he opened his eyes everything had gone and he was alone in a vast, echoing emptiness.

Chapter Twelve

Blind panic rooted Mark to the spot. 'All of it!' he had said. But he had meant the crystal prisms and the shining towers. This wasn't Brighton! It wasn't even a town! Fearfully he gazed around. Smooth walls sloped inwards and upwards and met high above his head. Far in front was a faint triangular glow. Behind, nothing but inky blackness. He was inside somewhere vast and dim. A cave? A vast, geometric cave? He couldn't be trapped inside one of the prisms – could he?

'Zip!' he whispered. 'Zip! Are you there?'

There was no reply.

'Zip!'

No sound but a strange, dull hum.

He didn't call again but moved slowly, cautiously, passing from darkness into light as he neared the entrance. A curtain seemed to be strung across it. A rough kind of netting pulled taut from three sides and gathered to a central point. The strands were thick but they didn't look very strong. He unclasped his knife. One hand for the knife; one to steady the cord. He stepped nearer – and instinctively recoiled. The cord was soft – and hairy – and warm.

The humming sound was getting louder. He traced it to where the threads gathered . . . to where a dark mass moved . . . and the sight turned his blood to ice. A giant spider was spinning her web.

Crooning gently, she fixed another strand. Then slowly, painfully, started on the long climb down. Mark didn't wait till she had finished. He turned and fled into the darkness. Spiders were things he dreamt about in his worst nightmares. Big, man-eating spiders . . .

He shut his eyes. 'It's only a nightmare!' he whispered. 'Only a dream. Soon I'll wake up and . . .'

But there was something different about this dream. He wasn't watching it. He was living it – and suddenly he knew that he wasn't going to wake up until he was out of the cave.

A soft, slithering sound was coming nearer and nearer. Was the spider coming to get him? He threw himself into the smallest angle between floor and wall. Would she drag him back to the web and suck out his juices? Or eat him then and there?

The sound stopped and his heart stopped with it. He tightened his grip on the knife and with a wild yell rolled over and raised his arm to defend himself.

But he had forgotten the sloping wall. The knife was knocked out of his hand. It clattered to the floor – and a small, frightened animal jumped clear and scuttered into the darkness.

Mark sprang up. 'Zip! Wait for me!'

For once the monkey obeyed him. Mark picked up his knife and looked towards the web. The spider hadn't come after him. Maybe she was too busy. Maybe she wouldn't notice a boy and a monkey . . .

He undid his sweatshirt and shoved Zip inside. 'Right! That should keep you safe for a while! Only a little while!' he said more gently. 'Zip. That's a good name for you. You un–zip bananas. You zip off. Now you're zipped in!'

The monkey complained loudly, but Mark kept tight hold of the jiggling bundle. He tied the drawstring tight and faced the light with both hands free.

But as he retraced his steps he realized with a sudden stab of fear that the cobweb was a lacy thing no longer. That it was fast turning into a dense hairy mat. He ran towards it. Now was not the time for caution. The spider was shutting out not only light but air. He could feel his face flushing as the fresh breeze died away and a strange smell made him nauseous as he fought for breath.

He peered up at the web. The spider was still busy. As far as he could make out she was turned away from him. Could she hear? Could she see? He grasped the knife in both hands and stepped up to the web.

'Now!' he whispered as he raised his arms.

The blade sliced through the hairy cords. He raised his arms and slashed again – and from each severed end a glutinous liquid oozed. The smell was incredible. Sweet and sickly. He held his breath and hacked and cut and tore. Gobbets of the stinking sap landed on his face. He could feel them dribbling down his neck. Soon hands and sleeves were covered in it.

The shock waves reached the spider. She shrieked and turned and raced to find the source. Mark could see the spinning hooks. The cruel beak-like mouth. The multi-lensed eyes. No question now of which way she was looking. The huge spherical body was coming straight for him.

The power drained from him. His arms hung limply by his sides. Nearer . . . nearer . . . He stood stock-still, unable to move. Unable to tear his eyes from that fearful sight.

She stopped and circled sideways. She was humming again. A strange, low-pitched song of triumph. She was getting ready for a meal.

'Out! Get out!' His brain was giving orders but

he couldn't make his limbs obey. The foul jelly was drying . . . glueing his arms to his body . . . securing his body to the mesh.

A coldness crept over his face and hands. Everywhere the sap had touched bare flesh. It was stiffening. Hardening. Soon he would be cocooned. Soon he would be fused into the web.

Another sound. Zip, chattering and scolding. A sharp, rackety sound that cut through his stupor. Move! Cut! Get out!

Sheer terror galvanized him into action. His legs were still free. He braced his shoulder against the web and pushed. The grey cords stretched and became thinner. Fluid gathered in little drops along the hairs. Now! he thought . . . Now! But when the strands finally broke the liquid congealed to make a network of new bonds.

The spider was on the move again. Humming. Gloating. Mark twisted round and set his back against the web.

'Break! Break, can't you!'

His strength was ebbing fast. He made one last effort, digging his heels into the ground and pushing his useless body backwards out of the cave. One step at a time. Leaning . . . straining . . . but still not free. The slender lines still held him as he forced his way out into the sunshine. They sparkled and glistened like strands of spun sugar – and like sugar strands they dried and became brittle and finally snapped.

The spider raged and wailed and her keening rent the air. But it was not her lost meal she was mourning; it was her broken web. She lifted each fragment and stroked the torn ends. Like a mother she pressed them to her and from her own body brought forth new strands to strengthen them. Gradually a deep throbbing replaced the cries of anguish and Mark broke the last of his drying bonds and stumbled out of the cave.

But not into a green world. Mark almost sobbed with disappointment. Now where was he? Had he escaped the spider only to find another nightmare? Sand. Everything was sand. He fell to his knees and dug at the stuff with his fist. Now what was he to do?

'Ouch!' Zip was jabbering and scratching and tearing at the imprisoning sweatshirt. Mark tore at the string, Did animals imagine things? Did they have dreams? Nightmares? Probably not. Lucky things.

'I suppose you're real!' he muttered grimly as Zip struggled free. The monkey screamed abuse at him and scampered off.

'Yes. I suppose you would be!' he shouted after the disappearing animal. 'I don't suppose I shall ever get rid of you!'

Chapter Thirteen

Mark turned slowly round. His heart was pumping and he could hardly breathe. No town. No buildings. No sign of life. Only the tracks of one small monkey heading into the distance.

Three hundred and sixty degrees. Back to where he had started. No trees. No valleys. No hills . . . No hills? He went round again. No vast triangular opening where a spider mended her web? Nothing. Just a featureless desert that seemed to go on for ever.

There were two suns in the sky but without reference points he had no idea which ones they were. Or which planet they were circling. He felt a cold sweat spread up his back as he scanned the curve of the far horizon. He was alone and there was nowhere to hide.

He stifled a sob as he began to run. How stupid he had been! Conjuring up chips and space cities. Thinking he had the power to make things appear and disappear! Showing off. Laughing because he was going to put one over on Martin. And all the time the joke had been on him. He hadn't been wielding the power at all. He'd been a plaything. A toy. A pawn in some game he didn't even understand.

He pulled the sleeves of his sweatshirt down over his hands. How could he have been so foolish? So big-headed? Why hadn't he realized he was meddling with a force so powerful that it could even make his nightmares come true?

Fear shuddered through him as he remembered the spider. His legs weakened and he nearly fell. No way of telling how far he had come. No way of telling how far he had to go. The desert stretched endlessly in front of him. Behind, his footsteps melted into the monotony of yellow sand. Nothing to run to. Nothing to run from. Nothing to do but run.

The wind was increasing steadily. Now it whipped the dunes and filled the air with driving sand. It was difficult to breathe without inhaling the stuff. He held a hanky over his face. The grit still stung his eyes but he no longer cared. Moving. That was all that mattered now. All he could do. He forced himself on.

Sand. Sand. And more sand.

A stitch made him catch his breath and he had to slow down. He drew the hood of his sweatshirt over his head and tugged at the zip. Zip. Where was the little monkey now? Should he try to follow him? Go forward? Back? Sideways? He looked for the scratchy paw prints but they had vanished. So had the horizon.

He smiled grimly. Hadn't he read somewhere that travellers perished in the desert because they lost all sense of direction? That was a laugh. He'd had no idea of direction in the first place. He was moving just because anything was better than keeping still.

He lurched off again. The desert was a miserable place. Bleak and cheerless and lonely. No chance of finding Col in this. Sand streamed across his face and he pulled his hood tighter and turned his back into the wind.

Then he undid the knot again. There was a sound. Something he almost caught . . . He closed his eyes and listened. Yes! There it was! A beat. A very faint beat. It was wild and distorted . . . but he was almost sure he heard music!

He stumbled towards the sound. A high note that swooped and dived . . . a clash that jangled in the air and teased his ears. A cloud of sand whirled round him and cleared as the wind died. He could hardly believe his eyes! Zip was crouched beside a small fire . . . and there, jog-trotting all round him, was Col!

Mark rushed towards him. He expected a welcome. Smiles and a handshake. At least a 'Glad to see you.' But Col just went on dancing and Mark was left stranded by the fire. Was he such an unwelcome g uest? Unexpected? Unwanted? He'd pinned so much hope on this meeting with Col . . . And now . . .

He sank to his knees. What was the point of trying any more? He was too tired. He'd done what he set out to do. Found Col. And now he was worn out. Legs aching. Feet aching. Sides aching. Head aching. Tears gathered in his eyes. After all that he'd been through . . . to be ignored like this . . . It was too much. It was all too much. He hunched over and dug his hands into his pockets.

The red thread on Monk's button-eye caught on a rough fingernail. He swallowed a sob. Monk and the white room seemed so far away. On the other side of a long day. The Park Keeper. The Policewoman. The Sanctuary. The spider . . . There were so many things he'd wanted to ask Col. So many questions that needed answering. But obviously Col didn't care. Didn't want to hear the questions? Didn't know the answers? Maybe all he could do was dance!

At last the tune came to an end. Col unbuckled his drum and laid it down with a sigh of relief.

'Getting too old for this lark!' he said as the cymbals crashed to the ground. 'Knees aren't what they were. Hungry?'

Mark nodded. He was too bitter to be polite.

'Thought you might be.' Col settled down against his drum and shook some small round buns from a leather pouch. 'Help yourself.'

Zip was already eating. Mark rolled the button-eye between his fingers and stared suspiciously at the pile on the tambourine.

'It's all right. They're quite real.' Col poured himself some water from an old army flask. 'They're car cakes. Good for travelling. There's water too if you're thirsty.' He talked as if Mark had just popped in for tea. And this was the man who was going to explain everything?

Mark sniffed. The buns smelt real enough. Looked real enough . . . And Zip didn't seem to have any doubts. He lifted one reluctantly to his lips and took a bite. It was moist and crumbly and slightly sweet – but what it actually tasted of he couldn't tell. Whatever it was, it was good. He put the button-eye back in his pocket. Perhaps things weren't so bad after all.

'Are you real?' he said, as he reached for another.

Col laughed. 'Oh yes, I'm real!'

'And I'm real. What else?'

'Not much, I'm afraid.'

Zip snatched a piece of car cake from Col's outstretched hand.

'Zip?'

'If you want him to be.'

'Isn't he yours?'

'Mine?' Col popped the rest of the car cake into his own mouth. 'No. He doesn't belong to anybody.'

Zip jumped up on to Col's shoulder. He seemed perfectly at home.

'He's like my toy monkey.'

'Monk?'

'Yes. How did you know that?'

'I am a Watcher.'

Watcher? Mark sat up. What was a Watcher?

'Watchers Observe,' said Col grandly.

Mark helped himself to some water. Surely the question had only been in his mind?

'And you've been watching me?' he said aloud.

Col nodded.

'All the time?'

Col nodded again.

'Then you know . . .' Mark leaned over. 'You can tell me what's happening, can't you?'

Col shook his head. 'Watchers Observe,' he said again. 'They Do Not Interfere.'

Mark put the cork back in the flask. This wasn't at all how he had imagined his meeting with Col.

'But if you've been watching all the time . . .'

Col unfastened his helmet. 'I don't get around as

much as I used to. I have to cover Na–Zed and Ar–zen and Cra. Though I must admit I've been spending quite a lot of time here recently.'

'Here?'

'A–Os. I've been spending quite a lot of time on A–Os. Another cake?'

'Thanks . . .'

A–Os? Where was A–Os? Where were Ar–zen and Na–Zed and Cra for that matter? Mark bit into the third car cake.

'Way out beyond your Galaxy,' said Col without looking up. 'Somewhere near Vecon.'

This time Mark was sure he hadn't spoken aloud. He looked across at Col, but Col was cleaning out his tin whistle.

'But what am I doing here?' he burst out.

'You're just – staying.'

'But who brought me? And why?'

No reply.

'Did you bring me?'

'Oh, dear, no!' Col blew through each hole in turn and then tapped the tube on his knee.

Mark felt like seizing the whistle and throwing it in the fire. Why wouldn't Col look at him? Why couldn't he get a straight answer? Why didn't Col realize how important it all was?

109

'I just want to know what's going on!' he said heatedly.

Col shook his head. 'You wouldn't understand,' he said kindly. 'You Earth People are a Very Immature Species.'

'Immature?' Mark could hardly believe his ears. 'You mean us? *Humans*?'

'An Undeveloped Civilization.'

'We're not undeveloped!' said Mark indignantly. 'We've got rockets and satellites and the space shuttle and . . .'

'Rockets! Space shuttles!' Col threw back his head and laughed. 'Mere toys!'

'They got us to the Moon!' Mark retorted. 'How else would you travel through space?'

For a minute it looked as if Col was going to say something important. Then he changed his mind and picked up the tambourine instead.

'Have another?' he said.

'No, thank you,' said Mark stiffly.

Col crossed his legs and closed his eyes. Mark gazed into the fire. He wasn't sure what to say next. Immature Species indeed! At least they would have helped if they'd seen someone in trouble. Had the rescue in the square just been another dream? Why hadn't Col rescued him from the spider? He wasn't sure if he liked this strange man after all.

'Is it you that's doing all this?' he asked after a while. 'You know . . . Brighton and everything? I know we're not really on Earth, but . . .'

Col opened his eyes again. 'I told you. I am a Watcher.'

Mark smiled grimly. That word again. He went on quickly before Col could get in his bit about not interfering.

'Well, if it wasn't you . . .'

Col helped himself to another car cake. 'This is A-Os,' he said through the crumbs. 'On A-Os, Thought Materializes.'

Mark frowned. He felt a bit stupid. How could thought materialize?

'You see what you expect to see.'

'Oh.'

Had he heard right? Did he dare ask Col to repeat it?

'You-see-what-you-expect-to-see!' said Col again – only this time he emphasized all the words.

Mark shook his head. Maybe Col was right. Maybe it *was* all too much for an Immature Species to understand. All the same. He'd got to try. He looked enquiringly at Col. Could Col interpret confusion?

Col smiled. 'This is a pretty dull place mostly. Nothing but sand. It's only when someone comes along expecting something that there's anything here at all.'

'You mean – I only saw what I was expecting?'

'Exactly.'

'But what does that mean?'

Col sighed and tried again. 'The Christmas trees and the food. You thought of food didn't you? And space cities?'

Mark got to his knees. '*Brighton?*' he said eagerly.

Col nodded.

'But I didn't get it right!'

'But you didn't know that!'

'I did once I had stopped taking the yellow pills!'

'Ah, yes!' Col permitted himself a small smile. 'That must have given the Osmids something to think about! Such a simple train of reasoning. You drop one of their 'Here and Now' capsules and don't have enough juice left to swallow it – so you don't! You lack the power to see through the yellow coating – so you break it open. You are frightened by what you see – so you throw it away! It's all far too simple for an Advanced Species like the Osmids!'

'Osmids . . .?'

'There you are then!' Col obviously thought he had explained everything. 'You saw what you expected to see! What you remembered of your planet. You can't blame the Osmids if you didn't remember it properly!'

'But . . . but who are the Osmids?'

'Osmids?' Col frowned. 'Na–Zed – Zedmids. A–Os –

Osmids. Didn't you learn anything at school?'

Mark sat back again. This was turning out to be a very uneasy conversation.

He took another car cake and tempted Zip on to his lap. He missed Monk.

Well . . . at least he'd been right about the pills. He stroked the silky fur. 'Here and Now'? Good name for them. Swallow – and that's all you could remember. Just here and now . . .

Zip settled down to sleep. Mark tried to remember the questions he'd wanted to ask.

'Robots?' said Col suddenly.

But Mark was getting used to Col's strange ways.

'The Assistants and the Bus Drivers. All the officials were Robots.'

'Robots?' Col laughed. '*Robots?*' He shook his head. 'Robots indeed!'

'Well – what would you call them?'

'Why do you have to call them anything?' Col sounded like one of Mark's teachers on a bad day.

Mark pushed the sleeves of his sweatshirt up to his elbows and took a deep breath. No good getting upset. He tried again.

'Were they the . . . the Osmids?'

'No. They were just something the Osmids used.'

'But why?'

'Why not? It's their planet! They can do anything they like!'

'But *why*?'

Col sighed. These Immature Species could be very irritating.

'To find out what you were thinking of course!'

Mark stared into the glow of the fire. Another thing right! He was feeling a *lot* better! Maybe he wasn't as stupid as he thought!

'Of course you're not!' said Col.

Mark made a face. Robots . . . Osmids . . . One sounded as bad as the other.

'But why use Policemen and Park Keepers and things? Why couldn't they just appear themselves?'

'Appear? The Osmids? How could they? They're nothing but brains!'

'Brains!' Mark looked up again. 'So what do they want with me? I'm not even clever!'

'Who said anything about clever? *You're* just part of the experiment!'

'Experiment? What do you mean?' Mark tipped the monkey off his knee as he sprang up. 'What experiment?'

'The Osmids' experiment, of course! Look – calm down. You're quite safe here.'

'But . . .'

'Well, at least stop prancing about. You're making Zip nervous.'

The monkey was sitting scratching itself. It didn't look in the least nervous.

Mark forced himself to stand still. It was all very well for Col to tell him to calm down. They weren't experimenting with him! Memories of animal rights posters welled into his mind. Monkeys in cages. Rabbits with their fur shaved off. Dogs . . . He shivered. The pictures had made him sick when he first saw them – how long ago? It felt like a hundred years.

'Won't you please tell me what's going on?' he pleaded. 'I came all this way to find you and . . .'

'Impossible,' said Col solemnly.

'But why?'

'Because you wouldn't understand. I've told you. You belong to a very Immature Species.'

'Then let me fetch Martin or one of the others . . .?'

'Martin?'

'My friend. The fat one with glasses. You must have seen Martin!'

'Well . . .'

'He's clever . . .'

Col shook his head. 'Look. I'm trying to tell you . . . I know it must be difficult, but it's all actually in . . .'

'You mean *you* don't understand either!'

'No, I do not mean that I don't understand!'

'I'm sorry,' said Mark humbly. 'It's just that . . . the more you explain, the less *I* . . . understand.'

Col sighed. 'Look, this is *far* too much for an Immature Species. And it's really a very minor problem.'

'Well, it's not minor to me!' said Mark hotly.

Col didn't reply.

Mark traced his name in the sand. He missed Monk. Why had he just brought the eye?

'I want to go home,' he said after a while. 'You can help me, can't you?'

'Watchers Observe. They Do Not Interfere!' said Col implacably.

'But helping's not interfering!'

'Isn't it?'

'You mean you won't!'

'I mean . . . Why do you keep telling me what I mean? Sometimes it's not what I mean at all!'

'Besides – you did interfere. You helped me when I got trapped in the square.'

Col blushed. 'Well, I don't know about . . .'

'I do! I'd never have found the Sanctuary if it hadn't been for you!'

'Sanctuary?'

'That's what I call it. The tile circle. You know. Under

116

the Telecom Tower? It's a safe place, isn't it? What . . . What's the matter?'

Col was no longer looking so smug and superior. He had jumped up and was pacing back and forth in front of the fire.

'What's the matter? Didn't you mean me to find it?' Mark felt in his pocket. 'I thought you'd left the bell on purpose!'

'Bell? What bell?' said Col, turning sharply.

'From the band! You know . . .'

'But I didn't leave a bell!' Col held out his hand. 'Show me!'

Mark passed it over.

'And what makes you think it's mine?'

For answer Mark pointed down to Col's feet. The strap was still fastened round his ankle and right at the front was a space with a long thread trailing.

Col pocketed the bell. Then he shook his head.

'Yes,' he said sadly. 'I'm getting too old for this lark. Can't even keep up with the mending. Letting bells drop off all over the place. Interfering with an Immature Species . . .'

'But you weren't interfering! You were helping!'

'It comes to the same thing.' Col sat down heavily and leaned against the drum. 'Watchers Observe. They're not supposed to get Emotionally Involved.'

117

Mark got down beside him and they sat together in gloomy silence. Col seemed to be growing older and older. His head dropped forward. His shoulders hunched over. Zip came back to him – but chose Mark's knee to sit on. There was an air of despair about the place.

Suddenly Col straightened up. 'The bell doesn't explain everything,' he said. 'How did you find me again? How did you find Zip?'

'Didn't you send him?'

'I certainly did not! Zip's his own master. No. There must be something else. Turn out your pockets!'

'My pockets?' Mark repeated stupidly.

'What's inside them?'

A knife. A torch. A hanky. A broken rubber . . .

'Is that all?'

Mark felt again. His trouser pockets this time. There was nothing in them but Monk's button-eye, still with its scarlet thread. He laid it down with the rest.

'What's that?' demanded Col fiercely.

'It's an eye. Well, a button really. It belonged to Monk. I . . . What are you doing?'

But Col had seized the button and was holding it up at arm's length and it was sparkling like a star. Even the two suns seemed dull in comparison. For a moment the light flared and then it died as Col brought the eye down and handed it reverently back to Mark.

'Now I understand,' he said. 'I was not the only one who helped!'

Chapter Fourteen

A cool breeze blew over the sand and Mark sat close to the flickering fire. There was a feeling of night about the place, despite the two bright suns. Col still wasn't very talkative but at least he didn't go on about Immature Species. If Mark asked a straight question he got a straight answer. All he had to do was think of the right question . . .

Col leaned forward to get another car cake and the drum rolled over with a loud 'Boom!' Zip woke up and clung to Mark.

'No . . . it's all right. All right now. . .' Mark comforted the trembling monkey. 'It's all right now . . .' The words his parents had used. Not the Father or the Mother but his real, remembered, parents.

'Is this . . . something to do with that other me?' he said suddenly.

He'd thought it was quite a good question. He certainly wasn't prepared for Col's reaction.

Col had just popped the last piece of car cake into

his mouth. Now as he tried to speak he choked on it and the words came out in a splutter. Zip leapt about a foot into the air and hid behind a pile of instruments and Mark rushed for the water bottle and stood wondering whether to slap Col's back or not. Was it permitted to hit a Watcher? He was relieved when the choking fit passed and Col was able to speak again.

'You . . . you *know* about him?' he gasped.

'Yes. Do you want a drink?'

'No . . . No, take it away! You actually know about him? How?'

'I had this dream,' began Mark. 'At least, I think it was a dream. I know I was home and . . . Hold on – are you all right?'

'Yes, of course I'm all right! Go on! You dreamt of home? You saw him?'

'Yes!'

'But . . .'

'Don't you believe me? There's been a swap and I'm in the wrong place. Is . . . is that what it's all about?'

Col paused as if unsure of what to say. Zip decided it was safe to go to sleep again. Mark stood on one foot and waited.

'Let me ask you a question,' Col said at last. 'Have you ever heard of changelings?'

'Sure! They're children who . . . you mean, he's a *changeling*?'

Col nodded.

'Changed with me?'

Col nodded again.

'But that's only in fairy stories, isn't it? They steal a child and put one of their own in its place . . . No, you're joking! There's no such thing as fairies!'

'The stories are true, Mark,' said Col gravely. 'But you are right. There's no such thing as fairies.'

'The . . . the Osmids?'

'They have been working on this for a long time. Perfecting their techniques. Learning from each failure. This time they think they will succeed.'

'But they always get found out, don't they?' said Mark hopefully. 'There's always something that's not right and . . .' His words died away. Hadn't he thought about that before? About Mark II not being too perfect? 'Someone will suspect, won't they? My own father and mother? They'll know. Surely they'll know it isn't really me?'

'Why should they? I told you; this time the Osmids really think they've got it right. This one looks like you, sounds like you – he even has your mind.'

'You mean he thinks like me?'

'No, Mark,' said Col quietly. 'I mean he is using part of your mind.'

Mark shuddered. Mark II using his mind? No. It was too horrible to think about. He traced an 'M' in the sand. He wished he hadn't left Monk behind. It was all very well the toy monkey being special. Something that impressed even Col. But it was something comforting to hold that he needed right now. Now the answers were beginning to seem more frightening than the questions.

So this was A–Os. And the Osmids had brought him. And they had been using his mind to make him believe he was still at home. And to help Mark II. So Mark II was a Changeling. He added an 'ark' to the 'M'. So what was he expected to do about it?

He dug a 'II' beside the 'Mark' and his fingers touched something hard. He scraped at the sand and the breeze strengthened and lifted the dust away. Blue tiles with strange markings . . .

'It's the tile circle, isn't it?' he said excitedly.

'Tile circle?'

'You know – the Sanctuary – under the Telecom Tower!'

'Was that where it was?' Col could be very irritating at times.

'And there's something special about it, isn't there?

The Policewoman – she walked right through me, and . . . I'll be all right now, won't I? I'll be safe here?'

Col gave him a long look. 'It is a time slip,' he agreed.

'And all I have to do is stay here! Stay put! They can't touch my mind in here, can they!'

Still that penetrating look.

'Well, what's the matter with that? It's all very well for you! I told you I'm not clever! Ask the teachers! Ask anyone! And the more you tell me the less I understand. A place where you have to expect something before you see it. Osmids who are nothing but brains. Changelings. A Mark II who is using my mind? How do you expect me to understand?'

Chapter Fifteen

Col watched as Mark sat with his head in his hands. Earth Creatures had the least developed minds in the whole universe, he thought, and yet, somehow, this one had managed to evade the Osmids and sabotage their latest scheme.

'How could there be two of us using the same mind?' said Mark suddenly.

'Because the Osmids have created a link between you. Your thoughts are being automatically transferred to – what did you call him?'

'Mark II.'

'Your thoughts are being automatically transferred to Mark II.'

'But that's impossible . . . isn't it?'

Col threw another stick on the fire.

'This is really very difficult,' he said tetchily. 'It's all *far* too advanced for an Immature Species.'

'And now? They've lost me, haven't they?'

'For a little while. Yes.'

That familiar cold feeling started to creep up the back of Mark's neck.

'What do you mean – a little while?'

'Well, you can't stay here for ever!'

Mark was furious to find that his eyes filled with tears so easily. He bent over and examined his shoelaces.

'This – Sanctuary – as you call it. It's only a small time slip. Just a place I use for resting in,' said Col kindly. 'It won't take the Osmids long to find it.'

'Oh.' Mark untied the laces and did them up again. So he wasn't safe after all. This was only a breathing space. The Osmids still wanted him. Still needed him. They were probably out there. Just waiting to close in . . .

'But they'll find you too, won't they?' he said, looking up.

'Oh, I shall be long gone.'

'Another time slip?'

'No.' Col stood up and brushed the crumbs from his coat. 'I might go to Cra. I haven't been there for a while. Yes. Cra would be the best place. Very pretty at this time of year.' He sounded as if he was getting ready for a holiday.

Mark tugged at the lace until it broke. 'Don't forget to send me a postcard!' he said sarcastically.

'Postcard? I don't think I know . . .'

'Oh, forget it. It was just a joke.'

'But you are not laughing!'

'Well – it wasn't that kind of a joke.'

'No wonder the Osmids are having trouble!' Col shook his head. 'Even the top layer of your mind seems to be . . .'

'Top layer?' Mark lost interest in the laces. 'What do you mean?'

'Oh, why did I ever get into this?' Col groaned. 'Why didn't I just leave you in the square?'

'But . . .'

'But I'll do my best!' He sighed and sat down again. 'The human mind is in layers.'

'I don't understand!'

'Think of an orange.'

'An orange? Why an orange?'

'There is the skin – and the pith – and the fruit. All different but all attached. All part of one whole orange.'

He paused and waited for a question but Mark was too confused to put his thoughts into words. Oranges? What had oranges got to do with anything?

'Earth Creatures only seem to use the outside layer,' Col went on. 'The part that is thinking now. The skin. You go round and round on the outside.'

'And the pith?'

'The pith is memory. Sometimes bitter. Things you

remember. Things you would rather forget.'

A sudden vision of the man-eating spider made Mark shudder. Huge and hairy. No. He didn't ever want to hear that humming again.

'But it's there, isn't it? The spider in your nightmare?'

Mark nodded.

'I don't know why they'd want that bit!' he said doubtfully. 'Why give my nightmares to Mark II?'

'They are part of you, aren't they?'

'I wish they weren't!'

'You see?' Col kicked the fire. 'You're all the same.'

Mark shielded his face from the sudden flame. 'Well, I don't like them! Mark II can have them and welcome! See how he gets on! No wonder we don't want to delve into the pith!'

'Yet that is the only way into the Earth Mind . . .'

'Earth Mind!' Mark sat up. 'What's that? Do I have one?'

Col frowned. 'Forget about the orange,' he said. 'It was only to explain about the layers. No. The Earth Mind is not yours alone. It is held in common by all the creatures of your planet. You don't use it. You mostly don't know anything about it. It's just *there*. A repository, if you like. Everything that has ever been learnt or thought or done on Earth is there. Every development. Every step on the path. It's what makes you human.'

'So . . . we know everything . . . but we don't know we know it . . .' Mark sighed. Would paying more attention at school have helped? Oranges . . . Layers . . . 'And that's the bit the Osmids want?' he said. 'The Earth Mind?'

Col smiled grimly. 'That's the part they will need to understand if they want to take over Earth!'

'But why don't they just invade us?'

'You don't listen, do you? I told you! The Osmids are nothing but brains. *Nothing!* They haven't any bodies to invade with! But if they could find a way into the Earth Mind . . .'

'. . . then they could take over our bodies without us knowing anything about it!'

'Exactly!'

Mark stared at him in horror. 'And they're doing this through me?'

Col nodded.

'But I don't know the way into the Earth Mind! I don't know anything about it!'

'Of course you don't!' Col kicked the fire and made the sparks fly. 'The only way into the Earth Mind is by being human. By doing all the normal everyday things humans do . . .'

'And that's why I had to go on believing I was at home in Brighton! So that I'd go on doing and thinking things as usual! Cinema on Saturday, football on Sunday! Even small things like cleaning my teeth or knowing the names of my friends . . .' Mark hesitated. 'Martin II? Was he doing the same?'

'No. I keep telling you . . .'

'But that's what they're trying to do with these – changelings – isn't it?'

'Yes! That's what they're trying to do.'

'But I still don't understand *why*! If they can materialize everything they need . . .'

'Everything they need – yes. Everything they want – no!'

Mark glanced up. Col's voice had changed. He seemed to have got older suddenly. 'Why is it never enough?' he cried.

Mark didn't know what to say. The question wasn't directed at him. The words had been flung out to the empty air and they hung there as if they were waiting for an answer. He looked over at the drum and wished that Zip would wake up and come over. Talking to Col could be very unnerving at times.

'Power, Mark. They want power!' Col's voice had become gentler but his eyes had lost none of their sadness.

'And I suppose they're starting with us because they think we'll be a pushover!'

'That is the assumption.'

Mark shuddered. 'But that's horrible! What a sneaky mean thing to do! They could change us completely! Goodbye mankind . . .'

'. . . and goodbye Ar–Zen and Na–Zed and Cra! If this works with one species it will work with all the rest!'

'But then there would be nothing left!' Mark jumped to his feet. 'Nothing really real! Only the Osmid Version!'

Chapter Sixteen

'Can't you do something about it?' Mark demanded.

'Watchers Observe. They Do Not Interfere.'

'But suppose they try and change you?'

'Impossible!'

'OK – supposing they manage to change everything else? You said just now how boring they are. A whole universe of Osmids? You wouldn't like that, would you!'

'It's not for us to like or dislike. Watchers Observe . . .'

'I wish you'd stop saying that!' Mark wanted to give Col a good shake but he didn't dare. He kicked the drum and woke Zip instead. 'The Osmids are interfering with us, aren't they? An Immature Species? An Undeveloped Civilization!' He kicked the drum again and the monkey gave up any attempt at sleeping and went to sit by the fire. 'At least we'd try to help each other. Try to fight back . . .'

'Fight the Osmids? The Earth Creatures? How?' Col gave a bitter laugh. 'You don't even know the Osmids exist!'

'I do!'

'But you are here on A-Os.'

'Then I'll just have to get back and warn them, won't I? It's no good expecting Martin or Phil or any of the others to do it! I tried to tell them something was going on but they wouldn't listen! Besides – they don't have Monk!'

'Look – I keep telling you . . .'

'No! I'll just have to go myself!'

Col shook his head. 'Impossible!'

'Why is it impossible? I got here, didn't I?'

'The Osmids brought you! You can hardly expect them to . . .'

'Well, there must be some way!'

'And even if you did get back; what good would it do? How could you make the rest of your people understand the danger?'

'But I wouldn't have to, would I?' Mark put both hands on the drumskin and silenced it. 'Didn't you say that everything became part of the Earth Mind? Everything any of us thought or did? Well, if I could just get away from A-Os. If I could just get back to Earth . . . Then surely all that's happened to me would become part of the Earth Mind! People wouldn't need to understand. Not with words anyway! And maybe one of the scientists or someone clever would pick it up and . . . You did say it would all be there, didn't you? Everything that's ever been learnt or done or anything?'

'Yes . . .'

'Well then! The question is: will you help?'

'I keep telling you. Watchers . . .'

'All right! You don't have to *do* anything. Just tell me if I'm on the right tack. You could do that, couldn't you?' He went on quickly before Col had a chance to speak. 'The Osmids can't see me in here, can they?'

'We are in a different time.'

'So perhaps they can't tell what I'm thinking either?'

No reply.

'Well, what I'm thinking is this. Mark II needs me. He needs my mind to tell him what he is doing. You did say they'd created a link, didn't you? And just for now that link is broken. OK. He might be managing on his own for a little while – but each day will get more difficult. And the longer he's cut off from me, the worse it will get. Sooner or later people on Earth are going to start wondering about him. Mum and Dad for instance. I may not be all that clever – but at least I'm not a zombie!

'And if they take him to the doctor – or a psychiatrist even! That would be worse! Minds are what psychiatrists know about! Surely that's the last thing the Osmids want? People tracing Mark II to them? No, they'd have to do something about that. And my guess is they'd bring him back here. I mean, they can't risk blowing him up or anything! And if I could find the exact spot, and if I was there, then perhaps we could swap over again! I don't know how, but – well, it's the only thing I can think of. We're linked and . . . Somehow we're like the two ends of a pulley: when one goes up the other has to go down!'

There was silence while Col scratched his head.

'I don't know . . .' he said at last. 'You're a completely Undeveloped Species and by rights . . .'

'But I'm not far out, am I?'

'Far out?'

'I'm not so far from the truth. It's something like that, isn't it?'

'Well . . .' said Col reluctantly. 'If you skip over the details of Complementary Wave Particles and take for granted all the advanced knowledge of the Space/Time/Relativity Ratio then . . . Yes. I suppose it is something like that! But there's no need to look so pleased with yourself. You've still got to find the exact place and . . .'

'But I've been thinking about that too and . . .'

'I don't see when! You seem to have done nothing but talk for the last ten minutes!'

Mark couldn't help grinning. He always did think

better when everything was rushing along together. It was the quiet empty spaces that defeated him.

'It's got to be one of the places I couldn't get into, hasn't it? They couldn't risk my finding the spot again, could they? I never saw inside any of the offices or factories – but on the other hand, nobody ever stopped me from trying. Not like Martin's Mother. She was really officious. And I've been wondering about that because she was usually quite nice. And now that I come to think of it – Martin and I used to play behind his house all the time! It was a sort of hill . . . Pope's Hill! Yes! Now I remember! There were huts and tank traps and a kind of concrete bunker – left over from the war, I think . . . Yes! We did something about it in our "Brighton at War" project! And right at the top was a radio mast . . . and *that's* where his watch was! That was the dare! It was quite a spooky place and . . .'

'Spooky place? Dare? What are those things? And what has Martin's watch got to do with it?'

'But don't you see?' Mark was so excited that he could hardly stand still. 'That last day – well, night actually – that's where I was! Under the radio mast at the back of Martin's house!'

'In the middle of the night?'

'We'd all been playing up there – and Martin suddenly said he'd hidden his watch somewhere and . . .

I *knew* there was something fishy about that watch!'

'Fishy?'

'Because he'd hidden it, don't you see? The Osmids got it wrong! He couldn't possibly have had it with him! And that was the dare!'

'Dare?'

'To go back in the dark and find it!'

'But why?'

'Oh, that was just like Martin. Always thinking up . . .'

'No. Why the watch?'

'It's one of those special ones that glow in the dark, of course! Anyway, we went into his house – we were going to watch the Chelsea-Millwall match – only his mother noticed that he didn't have his watch on and wanted to know where it was – and Martin, the idiot, had to go and say that *I'd* borrowed it and of course I didn't have it on me and by the time I'd made up some kind of story about it being at home she'd got the idea that there was something funny going on – I don't know how mothers always know that kind of thing – and we were all sent packing and Martin was sent to bed. She was really furious because it was an expensive watch and she'd only just bought it for his birthday. So after that I just *had* to go back and look for it!'

Col looked completely bewildered. 'And the Osmids are hoping to understand all this? I'm sorry for them!

Really sorry! Well, go on! What happened next?'

'I went home, went to bed, waited till it was dark – and then I went back. I expect the others did the same – only . . . I had Monk with me!'

'Ah! So that's how he got here!'

'Well . . . It was dark! And I thought . . . if I met anyone I could hide him under my sweatshirt. Anyway . . . There's a side entrance to the hill a little way down from Martin's in Manston Road, and I got in that way and climbed to the top. I wasn't really scared – but I wasn't looking forward to searching those bunkers. I thought Martin would have put the watch in the worst place he could think of, but he hadn't. It was hanging from one of the struts of the radio mast and . . . that's all I remember!'

Mark knelt down in front of Col.

'It was Monk, wasn't it?' he said slowly. 'If it hadn't been for him I would never have dropped the capsule or dreamt about my real home – or found you . . .'

Col stretched out his hand and ruffled Mark's hair.

'I'm glad you found me,' he said.

Mark was so surprised he nearly toppled over. A Watcher liking somebody? Surely that couldn't be right!

But Col was looking at him quite straight and serious. 'Why don't you just stay here and help me?' he said. 'I could do with some help. Someone to talk to. I don't cover a lot of ground these days – but I'm sure you would find it interesting.'

'But what about the Osmids?' Mark's voice had dropped to a whisper.

'Oh – we'd manage to keep one step ahead of *them* all right! A little time slip here – a change of character there . . . Besides. Once the Mark II project collapses they'll lose interest in you.'

Mark turned away and gazed into the fire. For a moment he was tempted. He really did like Col, for all his strange moods. And Zip. He liked Zip too. It would be fun to travel to Cra. To see Na-Zed and Ar-zen. Much easier than trying to outwit the Osmids. The man – and his monkey – and his boy.

It sounded good. Besides, he was tired of doing everything on his own. He'd tried to warn the others. It wasn't his fault if they hadn't listened.

A log shifted on the fire and Zip woke up, yawned, and settled down against Mark's leg again. Mark reached down and stroked him. If he hadn't taken Monk with him that night. If Monk hadn't somehow been brought up to A-Os with him . . . He felt the monkey quiver and watched him curl back into a tight ball. No. It was no good. None of the others had anything like Monk to protect them. They were still taking the 'Here and Now' pills. Still believing this was real. If they were ever going to be rescued, then it was up to him.

'I'm sorry,' he said, staring hard at the tiles. 'I really would like to stay with you, but . . . I've got to get home.'

'Right then!' Col was on his feet and strapping on his instruments. He whistled and Zip woke up and jumped on to his shoulder.

'So long, Changeling! Travel well!' Col held out his hand and Mark felt something small and cold drop into his palm. It was the little bell. He wanted to say something – but what was there to say? Col was already fading.

'Get back to Brighton, Changeling – and remember – it's a link . . . Find the link!'

Mark knelt in the tile circle. He felt very much alone. Col gone. Zip gone. He sighed. Col might at least have waited to see him off. Might at least have left Zip. No. Zip was too flighty. Too unstable. Not like Monk. He brought out the button eye and held it with the bell.

'Right,' he said. 'Brighton. I want to be back in Brighton!'

And slowly, imperceptibly, the tiles began to change. The burnt glaze cleared and the patterns shone through strong and bright within their rim of stone.

A helmet. And a dolphin. And a star.

Chapter Seventeen

Mark didn't know what to think. He was inside a building, that was for sure. Inside a large, circular hall. And the shining tiles were no longer bound by a rim of stones. Now they covered the whole floor.

There were no windows. Sunshine poured in through the diamond panes of an enormous dome high above him. Huge carved double doors divided the curved wall into quarters. Mark tried one but it was locked. All around, oil paintings of solemn men hung in gilt frames. Some wore watch-chains. Some held scrolls. All stared into the middle of the room. Straight at Mark. He moved uneasily, looking for a place to hide but there were no corners and only a large round table offered any cover.

He tried another door. And another. Only the fourth door was unlocked. He stared across a courtyard to a broad street. It looked like Western Road. The same skyline. The same wide pavements. He recognized the entrance to the arcade and the little bay windows above the chemist. But there was no Marks and Spencer. No Wallis. No Starbucks. Instead, small shops half-hidden by sandbags. They didn't even have their names spelt out in lights. Just painted above the windows in plain gold letters. The Sweet Shop. Jas. Brown. Provision Merchant. The Maypole Dairy.

He looked up at the sky. Two suns were hovering above the horizon. Yes, it was Brighton all right. The Osmid Version. But was it night? Or day? He had no idea.

He walked across the road. The lamp standards had the usual turquoise dolphins twining around them – but the oblong sodium lamps had been changed for delicate glass globes and none of them were lit. He didn't notice the metal rails till he had nearly tripped over them. Railway lines in the middle of the street? And rows of wires above them? It was all very confusing.

He turned back to look at the place he had just left. It should have been the shopping centre but he was hardly surprised when it wasn't. No Smiths. No Dixons . . . No Telecom Tower. Just one enormous grey stone building with tall arched windows and a clock tower at one end. Nearly ten o'clock. But night? Or day? He still wasn't sure. He half expected the clock to chime, but it didn't. Behind it, the sea shone calm and blue. That was another surprise. You couldn't usually see the sea from Western Road.

Usually he would have taken a bus to Martin's house, but there was no sign of traffic. He'd have to walk. Streets didn't change, did they? He only had to keep going down North Street, fork left at the bandstand, up through the Terraces, and there you were at Pope's Hill. He'd done it dozens of times.

He hesitated. Home was in the opposite direction. No. Better not to think about that. Better not to think about anything the Osmids might latch on to. If all this worked he would be home soon enough. Really home.

There were no shadows but he kept close to the side of the buildings all the same. He couldn't understand why there were no people around. Still. It made things a whole lot easier. No one to ask what he was doing. No Robots to avoid. He frowned. No wonder he had felt uneasy when Officials were about. All that smiling. Probing. And all the time . . . No. Best to keep away from them. Best not to think too much.

The bandstand was down on the Steine. Mark remembered it as a forlorn place standing in a weedy flower-bed at the junction of three main roads. Every spring the council workmen gave it a coat of paint – and every summer it looked just as grimy as ever. It certainly wasn't much use as a bandstand. Even if you could reach it through the six lanes of traffic, you wouldn't be able to hear anything! Cars . . . lorries . . . motorbikes . . . buses . . . They all went round it in a never-ending stream.

But not today. Today everything was quiet. And as Mark came down the hill he could see that the Steine was completely different. The roads had shrunk and the gardens had grown. Now the bandstand was the centrepiece of a small park with smooth lawns and proper flower-beds and clumps of trees. There were even paths across it, linking the Old Steine with the new.

He hurried over. Not all of the lawns were smooth. Under the trees, one of them rose into a strange hump. An ancient barrow? It looked a bit like an ancient barrow. Long and oval and covered with turf. But the turf was new-laid – and the steps that led down to the entrance were made of concrete – and there were more sandbags. Always sandbags. He'd never seen so many. There was a sign with a big red 'S' on it too. No! It definitely wasn't an ancient barrow!

'It's a . . .' Mark began. And then a loud descending scream made him catch his breath as four planes came out of the clouds.

'Stukas!'

He shielded his eyes. Out over the sea more planes, JU 87s, were diving at an unseen target. His mouth fell open and he blinked several times but nothing changed. And then he remembered. This was what he had written about in his 'Brighton at War' project. The public shelters in the gardens. The aerial battles over the town. No wonder it was all so strange and yet so familiar! He had materialized Brighton all right – but Brighton of World War II! But how . . .? He fingered Monk's eye. Another little time slip?

How long would it take the Osmids to find it? Not long. They must have known about it the minute it appeared. But understand? How could they understand! Only someone who had been in Miss Ritchie's class could hope to understand it all in one go! All those weeks talking about 'Brighton at War'? Acting out air raid drill. Living on rations. Looking at gas masks and ration books and identity cards and old money . . . Oh, yes! He, Mark, understood! And so long as they didn't find him too soon . . .

'Good job I landed in the middle of an air raid,' he thought. 'The Osmids won't know anything about fire watching or ARP Wardens or WVS!'

A burst of gunfire made him jump. 'It's so *loud*,' he said to himself. 'I know it's coming from the Downs – but I didn't realize it would be so *loud*! Oh, if only Martin was here!' he whispered, as another wave of planes flew low overhead. They'd talked about this so often. Envious of the boys who had watched dog-fights over the Channel. Who had explored bomb sites and shot-down planes. Picked up shrapnel or old bullets. Martin had some bits of Spitfire his uncles had found – but it wasn't the same as finding something yourself! Hot shrapnel or newly fired shells!

'And won't he be jealous if I get some!' Mark muttered as he turned to watch a group of British planes coming over from the west.

'Hurricanes and Spitfires! Probably been scrambled from Tangmere . . .' He was so excited he hardly realized he had spoken aloud.

'Rubbish!' said another voice. 'No Spitfires at Tangmere! They've come from Biggin Hill or Kenley . . .'

'Martin!'

But there was no time to ask how Martin had managed to get there. The Spitfires were diving down on the enemy planes and the tight formation was breaking up and heading out to sea. The boys were still arguing as they ran down towards the pier.

'Messerschmitts!'

'No way! JU 87s!'

'I'm telling you, it's BF 109s!'

'I can't see . . . They're flying out over the Channel . . . Do you think it's the attack on the convoy?'

But there were wooden barriers and coils of barbed wire all across the forecourt of the pier and a large plank with 'Restricted Area' splashed across it in red.

Mark hesitated.

'Not scared of a bit of old wire, are we!' sneered Martin.

Martin had a way of sneering that usually made Mark do all sorts of stupid things. But not today.

'Come on!' he shouted as he ran back past the Aquarium. 'Let's get up on Pope's Hill!'

Once across Marine Parade there was a maze of little streets to get through. He ran up Wentworth Street . . . turned into St James . . . into Upper Rock Gardens . . . across Edward Street and into Egremont Place. He was nearly through Park Hill when he realized he was on his own. Martin was still puffing up Egremont Place.

'Hurry up! It'll be all over and we'll miss it!'

But Martin wasn't hurrying. He sat down on a low wall. 'Why can't we go by bus?' he whined.

'Because there's an air raid on!'

'But we usually take a bus!'

'No buses . . . Don't you remember? We read all about it for our "Brighton at War" project.'

'But that was in books! I can't walk all that way!'

'You could if you weren't so fat . . .'

147

'Fat nothing! I'd rather go down on the beach and collect shrapnel.'

'The beach is mined! Don't you remember?'

A barrage of gunfire made them jump.

'Ack–Ack guns! Probably from the top of the hill!' said Mark. 'Come on! We're missing it all!'

Martin followed unwillingly.

'Nearly . . . there . . .' Mark turned into Freshfield Place . . . into Craig Terrace – and for a moment he wondered if he was back in his own time. Three windows. Two up, one down . . .

Into Beverly Terrace . . . Anstruther Terrace . . . Pot plants in the windows. Bamboo blinds . . . But the windows had some kind of diamond pattern pasted over the glass. Mark grinned. No. This wasn't his own time. These were the 'Air Raid Precautions' he had read about. He wondered if it was worth saying something about it to Martin, but Martin was having enough trouble finding the breath to climb hills. He had none to spare for clever arguments.

Still no people. No Fathers taking dogs for walks. No Mothers chatting over garden walls. No Robots? Mark shuddered. How long did an air raid last? How long did a time slip last? How long before the Osmids worked out where he was?

A shell zinged overhead.

'*Get down!*'

But Martin was already down. They crouched together beside one of the low walls. They could see the star-burst of the exploding shell above the houses and one of the paper-pasted windows crumpled inwards.

'Wow!' Martin stared in amazement. 'Did you see that!'

Mark hid a smile. Maybe now Martin would get a move on!

Another burst of Ack-Ack fire from the Downs. It was difficult to make out the trace of bullets in the light of the bright suns but they could see the vapour trails as two engaging planes fought to gain height.

Mark was too excited to stay down. 'It's a dog-fight! A real dog-fight!' he shouted as he jumped up and ran into Holly Lane.

Holly Lane was narrow and muddy but it led straight into Manston Terrace and the side entrance to Pope's Hill. Unfortunately, it also led straight into the arms of an official-looking lady with a notebook in her hands and a WVS hat on her head.

The lady recovered first.

'What's your name, boy?' she demanded. 'And where's your label?'

'I'm . . . I'm looking for it . . .' Mark wriggled and

squirmed but she had him by the sleeve.

'You should have been evacuated. You've no right wandering around here. What's your name?'

'John! It's John . . .'

'No, it isn't!' Martin had puffed up the lane and was coming towards them.

'Another one! Where's your label, boy?'

'He's Mark Asher and he lives in . . .'

'Shut up!' Mark aimed a kick at the thick-stockinged legs and the lady shrieked and let him go.

'Run!' He seized Martin's hand and ran. The WVS woman was a Robot all right. But how had they found him? He pulled the protesting Martin round the corner into Manston Terrace. Martin lived at number fifty-two. If only they could get there before the WVS Robot recovered.

Chapter Eighteen

'Wh . . . what did you do that for?' Martin was sobbing with exertion.

'Don't stop! I'll tell you later! We've got to get into your house . . .'

'But the Mother's out and she doesn't like . . .'

'It doesn't matter. Come *on*!'

Number fifty-eight . . . fifty-six . . . fifty-four . . . Martin's house.

'It'll be locked . . .'

But Mark was already half-way up the path to number fifty-two. Still no sign of WVS.

'Doesn't she keep an emergency key under the windowsill?'

'Yes, but . . . you're not supposed to know about that . . .'

Mark poked his finger into the hole and hooked the key out. '*Everyone* keeps a spare key under the windowsill!' He unlocked the door and pushed Martin into the house.

'Wh . . . what's happened . . .'

Even Mark was taken aback for a minute. No carpets. No furniture. The place was empty. Then he remembered. During the war these houses had been requisitioned. They were all empty. Everyone had gone. He looked at the sobbing Martin. Martin didn't like it when he didn't know what was happening. But how could he explain?

'It's wartime . . .' he began.

'No it's not! It can't be . . .'

'Look. I've no time to explain it to you right now! See if old WVS is in sight yet.'

'You were rude to her! You didn't even give the right name! The Mother says you must always pay attention to people in authority . . . And you *kicked* her!'

Mark groaned. Martin wasn't going to be much help. 'I've got to see what they're doing on the hill!' he said sharply.

He rushed through to the empty scullery and looked out.

Pope's Hill looked like a massive building site. The bunkers were already taking shape and a huge gun emplacement had been hacked out below. He could even see the guns ready to be hauled into place. Right opposite was the entrance to a tunnel. Still not a soul in sight.

'I suppose the tunnel's a sort of shelter . . . Maybe there's a Command Centre down there! Strange that we didn't know anything about it. Even Miss Ritchie . . .'

'No wonder the Mother said we weren't to go there!'

'Martin . . .' Mark began. And then he noticed something. The radio mast was missing. Had that been put up during the war? Or long after? And did it matter? He sighed. Surely if he just got to the bunker . . . but how? Still no one in sight – but if old WVS was a Robot, you could bet there would be others along.

He looked at Martin. Funny that he had always thought Martin was so great. Clever. Smart. That kind of thing. But no use now. He didn't know enough to keep away from the windows.

'Who's that?'

'Where?'

'There . . . with the dog.'

Mark squinted sideways to see where his friend was pointing. Oh, yes! It was a Robot all right! Dressed like an Army Officer with a shining brown belt and brown boots. And he was coming straight for the back fence of fifty-two. 'Get down!' he hissed.

'Why?'

'Don't argue! Just do it!' He pushed his friend down behind the sink.

'Come out, boys!' called the Officer.

'We'd better go . . .'

'Not likely!'

'But they know we're here!'

'So whose fault is that?'

'Mark Asher! I know you're in there! I want to talk to you!'

'He only wants to talk!' whispered Martin.

'I'll bet!' Why on earth had Martin told WVS his right name?

'The Mother says you should always do what those in authority tell you!' And Martin got to his feet and leaned towards the window as if he was going to knock on it. Luckily the man was busy unleashing the dog and Mark managed to pull his friend down again before he noticed.

The dog pushed through the broken fence and sniffed among the blackcurrant bushes. Mark wasn't very sure about Alsatians. Still, it couldn't get into the house.

But it wasn't just the dog. Something else was searching. Something that didn't stop outside. Something that came right through the walls of the scullery and into his mind. It was like the Park Keeper all over again. He could feel it probing. Feel it trying to make some kind of connection. Feel it trying to link up. No. The dog didn't need to come in.

He put his hand in his pocket and found Monk's eye. And almost before he knew what was happening he found himself counting aloud.

'Two . . . four . . . six . . . eight. Two . . . four . . . six . . . eight. Two . . . four . . . six . . . eight. Two . . . four . . . six . . . eight.'

'What are you doing?'

'Counting! Building some kind of shield in my mind! Come on! Count! Start on the multiplication tables. You remember multiplication tables? Two times two is four . . . two times three is six . . . two times four is eight.'

Martin looked at him as if he was mad. 'What for?'

Mark didn't stop to answer. He went right on through the tables. 'Six times three is eighteen . . . six times four is twenty-four.' He prodded Martin. 'Six times five is thirty . . .'

But Martin was having none of it. 'You're crazy!'

Mark nodded and grinned.

The officer was still standing at the end of the garden but he looked puzzled.

'Nine times four is thirty-six, nine times five is forty-five . . .' Mark chanted on. So Martin thought he was crazy! So what? He would understand once it was all over. 'Nine times six is fifty-four, nine times seven is . . .' He could keep this up all day if necessary.

There was a loud whistle. The dog ran back through the fence and the Officer moved away.

Mark ran some water in the stone sink and splashed his face.

'You're crazy!' said Martin again.

'It worked, though, didn't it! Fancy multiplication tables coming in useful! Well, Miss Ritchie always said they would!' He squeezed the button-eye. Martin might not be any use – but he was not entirely on his own! He looked around for a towel but there wasn't one. He dried his face on his hanky.

'Can't you just tell me what's going on?'

'Well . . .'

But the sound of hammering took him through to the front room. Soldiers were fixing great planks of wood across the doors and windows. More hammering. The back this time. Two more soldiers were boarding up the hole in the fence.

'No time now . . .'

'But they're shutting us in!'

'Shhh!'

The men marched off. They hadn't looked like Robots. Just ordinary men. Not like the Officer, inspecting the fence as if he didn't expect the work to be done properly. At last he too moved away.

'We're shut in!'

'Oh, don't be stupid! Don't you remember the loose plank in the corner? Come on!'

Mark opened the back door.

'No! The Mother says we mustn't . . .'

'*Yes!*'

Mark pushed his friend through the hole in the back fence. It wasn't easy but at least Martin seemed to have given up arguing about everything. He took his friend's hand and ran towards the bunkers.

Suddenly, the four Stukas screamed out of the clouds again.

'Run!'

The planes were coming straight at them. Bullets rained on to the ground in front of them. He pulled Martin sideways and tried a different tack. But the planes were taking it in turn to dive, and each dive meant another hail of bullets across their path.

Mark ducked and dived and zig-zagged and Martin sobbed and whined behind him.

'It's all your fault!'

'Martin . . .' He took a tighter grip on Martin's hand. '*Move!!!*'

But whichever way Mark turned, a hail of bullets shot up lines of dust in front of them.

'It's not real,' he kept telling himself. 'It's not real . . .' But it seemed real enough. The scream of the diving planes . . . the sharp bark of the guns . . . the smell . . . the sting of stone fragments when he didn't dodge quickly enough . . .

He wanted to run away. To wake up. To throw himself down on the ground and cover his head. Anything to escape the relentless attack . . . but they weren't at the bunkers yet. He couldn't stop until they had reached the bunkers. Only a few more yards . . . Only a few more seconds . . . He dragged Martin behind him. Maybe when they reached the shelter of the bunkers the Stukas would give up . . .

But they didn't.

The bunkers hadn't been completed yet. No protecting doors. No comforting tunnel to run into. The boys crouched behind some reinforced concrete but the Stukas changed tactics and started to come in low and straight at the entrance. Dive after dive. Scream after scream . . .

'Make it go away. Please, please make it go away . . .' Martin was really crying now. Really frightened.

Mark tried to think. They'd made it to the bunkers. Made it back to the place where he'd found the watch. Back to where his part in the Osmid Version had started. So why didn't he just . . . make it all stop? He'd had enough of being shouted at and hunted and being a target. No. He shuddered.

'Brighton at War' had never been like this.

Was it worth trying to explain it all to Martin first? Probably not. They'd have plenty of time when they were back in the real Brighton.

'OK,' he said. 'I'll make it disappear.'

'No!'

Mark looked at his friend. He really was a wimp!

'It's all right,' he said soothingly. 'I've done it before. You can hold my hand if you're scared.' Martin stared at him – but he held out his hand.

'Brighton at War!' Mark said loudly. 'I don't want it any more!'

But nothing happened. The Stukas came out of the clouds for another attack. Cockpits gleamed in the light of the two suns. Sirens screamed as the attack went on.

The familiar cold fingers of fear started to creep up the back of Mark's neck. He took a firmer hold of Martin's hand. It was moist and sweaty.

He shut his eyes. 'Everything that isn't real,' he said loudly, 'I want it to go away! *Everything!*'

There was a sudden silence and a cool sea breeze wafted across Mark's face. Had he done it? Had he really got rid of the Osmid Version? He gave Martin's hand a squeeze of triumph – and opened his eyes in panic.

'Martin!' he shouted into the empty air.

But there was no reply.

'Martin!' he yelled again.

But Martin was nowhere to be seen.

Mark turned slowly. There was no bunker. No row of terraced houses. No Brighton. No sign of life. Only the same featureless desert where he had found Col. Three hundred and sixty degrees. No gun emplacements. No noise. No Stukas. No Martin.

'Martin?' he whispered.

And then he remembered. 'Everything that isn't real' he had said. But he had meant the air attack and the war and the bullets and the . . .

And suddenly he knew. He didn't need the prickly sensation to warn him. He knew it all at once and as surely as if he had heard Col say the words.

Martin hadn't been real either.

Chapter Nineteen

Mark stood where he thought the bunker had been and somehow knew that he was not alone. The two suns faced each other across the sky and his shadow was long and low. But the boy beside him cast no shadow. Mark II stood like a pale reflection waiting for his mirror-twin to turn.

Fair hair. Grey eyes. Blue jeans. Grimy sweatshirt. Dusty trainers. They were alike in every detail. Even down to the rip on the sleeve. Mark knew there was something he should remember about that but memory was fading fast.

He'd always imagined Mark II as less than human. A Robot like the Officials. But here he was, standing in the sandy desert of A-Os and looking worried and excited and frightened all at the same time. Looking exactly as he himself felt.

What should he say? 'Hello'? 'Goodbye'? How did you tell yourself to go away? Or might he tell you? What if you both said the words at the same time? The two boys faced each other and neither of them smiled.

Mark sighed. What a desolate, barren, miserable place . . . What a place to call home! He glanced surreptitiously at his twin but there was no answering sigh.

He doesn't know what I'm thinking about! Doesn't really know what 'home' means or what is happening! He's not Mark! I'm Mark – and *I'm going home!*'

In spite of himself, Mark smiled. He raised one hand and like a mirror-image, Mark II did the same. There was no need for words. Eyes met. Palms touched. There was a tingling sensation somewhere inside his head and suddenly he was alone. No twin. No Mark II . . . From long ago he heard Col calling in farewell. But already he was travelling through the deep of space. The last goodbyes faded away unanswered.

Faster and faster through the dark. Speed dazed his senses – and yet it seemed as if he was suspended in a void. Were speed and stillness the same thing? He shut his eyes tight.

And then a dog barked and his eyes shot open. He was standing on firm ground. Standing on the damp grass of his own front lawn with the fronds of the pampas-grass swaying and rustling in the starlight.

He shivered. His feet were cold. He couldn't think what he was doing fully dressed on the lawn in the middle of the night. Sleep-walking? It was a long time since he had done that. He just hoped he hadn't banged the front door and locked himself out again.

The house was dark and he had to feel his way upstairs. He avoided the squeaky step. No point in waking the parents; they'd only worry. He tiptoed along the landing to his own room, took off his clothes and got into bed. It was still warm.

Monk toppled off the headboard and rolled down beside him. Poor old Monk. He didn't get much cuddling these days. Mark sighed and put him back on his perch. His father was right. He was too old for toys. Time to give Monk to Oxfam.

He settled himself down to sleep. Saturday tomorrow. No school. He'd meet Martin in the morning. See what was on at the pictures. Then in the afternoon they could go to the park or maybe just hang around town. That was the best of Brighton. Always something going on. Perhaps they'd meet that one-man band again. He had a monkey. A bad-tempered little beast who collected money and spat at people. Not a bit like Monk.

He reached up and retrieved Monk from the headboard. The tickle of fur was comforting against his neck. He pulled the old toy under the covers. Oh well . . . so long as nobody found out.

He turned on his side and wrapped his arms around Monk's battered body and went to sleep.

Author's Note

If you go to Brighton you will find the Palace Pier and the Pavilion and the Brighton Centre and Marine Parade exactly where you would expect to find them. There is even an old, unofficial coat of arms for the city with dolphins and a helmet and a star.

But the bandstand? And the scented garden? And the circle of tiles? And the bunkers left over from the war? Every one of them is there all right – but not quite as Mark remembered them.

And as for the open-air shopping centre at Churchill Square . . . and *The Spirit of Brighton* . . . and the Telecom Tower . . . I'm afraid they were pulled down long ago.

But then, it wasn't really Brighton at all, was it? Only the Osmid Version!

THE BOXES

William Sleator

'And don't *try to open them. Don't even* think *about trying to open them,' Uncle Marco said. 'I'm leaving them with you because you're the only person here I can trust. No one else can even know they exist.'*

Annie has enough to worry about without Uncle Marco's boxes. Her Aunt Ruth is always in a vile mood, her best friends are smitten with each other, and, worst of all, the Crutchley Development Company is after the family home.

But the boxes have a hold on her, peopling her thoughts and dreams with their mystery . . .

Until down in the basement amidst the dust and spiderwebs, she decides one day to take a look . . .

OWL LIGHT
A W H Smith Mindboggling Book

Maggie Pearson

Hal stood at the window, watching the darkening sky. Beyond the twilight lay a different world. A world where things changed their shape and creatures lurked that never saw the light of day. Where imagined fears took shape from the shadows and lived a life of their own.

Hal has always been scared of the dark. The villagers' tales of werewolves roaming the common are no help at all. It is a wild, forbidden place – a place of mysterious sounds, home to threatened badgers, and the haunt of intriguing neighbours . . .

And then Hal's sister Ellie starts disappearing at night . . .

OMEGA SEVEN

Maggie Pearson

Omega Seven. The Paradise Planet. No pollution, no poverty, no crime . . . no worries.

And – as far as Luke is concerned – no fun. Omega Seven could be just about the most boring planet in the Universe.

Except for the mysterious Blue Mountains. The gateway to another world entirely. A world where nothing is *quite* what it seems. And this one isn't nearly as boring . . . or safe.

Who can he trust, and where will his journey end?

'. . . fast-paced, cliff-hanging action . . . Recommend this one.' *School Library Journal*

DEAD EDWARD

Stephen Moore

My name is Edward. Edward Gwyn Williams. I'm a schoolboy. I'm fourteen years old, near enough. Let me tell you something — I will always be a schoolboy. I will always be fourteen years old. I AM DEAD.

When Edward trips over his home-made Guy Fawkes one night and hurtles to the bottom of the stairs, he doesn't know that this action will be his last. But Edward must come to terms with being a ghost — dressed for all eternity in a grubby t-shirt and his sister's fluffy slippers! Then he meets the other ghostly inhabitants of 13 City Road — and discovers that being dead is the very least of his worries . . .